D0674054

The Fabulous Manticora

The Fabulous Manticora

JOSEPHINE LEE

Jonathan Cape Thirty Bedford Square London

FIRST PUBLISHED 1973
© 1973 BY JOSEPHINE LEE

JONATHAN CAPE LTD, 30 BEDFORD SQUARE, LONDON WCI

ISBN 0 224 00849 8

PRINTED AND BOUND IN GREAT BRITAIN
BY W & J MACKAY LIMITED, CHATHAM

Apollonius asked "if they had
   among them the Mantichora".

"What!" said Iarchas, "have you
   heard of that animal; for if
   you have, you have probably
   heard something extraordinary."

"Great and wonderful things I have
   heard of it," replied Apollonius.
   "It has a head like a man's, is as
   large as a lion with a tail from
   which bristles grow, which it
   shoots forth like so many arrows
   against its pursuers ... "

"Mantichora ... bestia horrenda"
   (A brute fit to give one the horrors).

LEIGH HUNT, *Autobiography*

7

George was unhappy. He didn't know why and that made it worse. There wasn't a special reason, or even a definite feeling. Everything was rotten. Although he had kicked the stone from the gutter along two streets and round a corner without missing once, he stayed in the same mood. His mother wasn't her usual take-it-or-leave-it self either. She was nervous. George found it was catching and that bothered him, partly because he liked to think that nothing ever rattled him, and partly because this was the first time he had ever seen his mother in a dither of uncertainty. He wasn't like the kids (four younger brothers) never expecting Mum and Dad to put a foot wrong. He was old enough to realize they had their worries and were a long way from being in command of themselves, let alone their large family. Dad let you see this sometimes, but Mum always made you feel everything would come right in the end.

She could be good company – for a mother. George knew he was the one she liked best, though she never *said* anything or acted soft. It ought to have been Polly, who was the only girl and the oldest, but she was Dad's favourite. Or used to be. George and Mrs Fowler enjoyed an outing together, as a rule, sharing jokes and poking fun at Dad, who was an old stick-in-the-mud, and at Polly, now she acted the great lady since she had married into the cream of society. That was only one of their jokes, but this afternoon George and Mrs Fowler were both wishing they were somewhere else with someone else, and it was Polly's fault.

They stood at the bus stop in silence. Mrs Fowler was wrapped in her own thoughts. It made George feel lonely. He actually took hold of the stuff of her coat and pulled at the sleeve.

"Do we really have to go, Mum?"

"Oh, George. I've already explained. It's for Polly's sake."

"I don't see why you and me must go to a tea-party at the Sheldrakes just because our Polly's married their Matthew."

"It's not a party, George. It's just us to tea with Matthew's mother. There probably won't be anything to eat, except perhaps a biscuit."

George felt even more melancholy and mutinous.

"Why can't you and Dad go to supper or dinner or something? I expect they have cocktail parties every night. Why does it have to be me?"

"We were invited. Dad refused. Some people might have taken offence. Any of us are lucky to be asked a second time."

"Oh are we."

But George didn't say any more. His mother was too jittery this afternoon to be chivvied.

"Does Dad know we're going?" he asked, after a short, miserable silence.

"No."

Mrs Fowler tried to sound as if she couldn't care less. George wasn't taken in. He whistled.

"But what'll happen if Dad comes home first, before us, and the kids are yelling for *their* tea. They'll be ravenous as well – out to play all the afternoon. Why couldn't Mrs Sheldrake have asked the whole lot of us? She must know we all have half-term together."

"That sort of thing never enters her head," Mrs Fowler replied. "And think what you're saying, George. Imagine the four of them letting rip amongst that valuable china and glass. *I'd* have heart failure even if she didn't. Don't worry about Dad. Polly's promised to pop in and cook their tea and Matthew will pick her up later. They're eating out at some new restaurant Polly's heard of, so she's nothing else in the world to do until then."

Mrs Fowler paused, suddenly stricken at the thought of all the odd jobs waiting for her that evening. Then she added, rather sadly,

"Polly's the only one who can manage your father."

"Dad's never got over her going off and getting married in secret to a complete stranger the minute she was eighteen, has he?" George asked sympathetically. Usually, when his mother was under the weather, George purposely made light of everything. Most times it worked, but this afternoon he didn't feel like being amusing and he sensed that his mother wouldn't be easy to cheer up. "It's not fair, really," he continued, still serious, "Dad being so down on Matthew. After all, Matthew kept it a secret from his parents as well."

"Never you mind about that."

George was really angry. What was the use of trying to be sympathetic and serious, when you were shut up as if you were a baby? Mum wasn't ever like this -- she always let you enter into the spirit of whatever she was thinking about or talking about. He'd rather be angry than unhappy, though.

"But I do mind," he continued, in his playground-fighting voice. "I mind a lot if it means dressing up in this revolting tweed jacket and flannels and wearing this horrible tie, and spending my half-term sucking up to Mrs Sheldrake just because Dad's too proud to have anything to do with them because he thinks they'd turn their noses up at him."

George paused for breath, but Mrs Fowler wasn't going to be provoked.

"How can he tell if no one tries to be friends?" she asked reasonably. "They might be very nice when we know them."

"Then why doesn't Matthew like them? He's known them long enough. He says his mother and father are a pair of antiquated snobs."

"You could say the same for your dad – they might get on like a house on fire," Mrs Fowler said with a wry smile.

George wasn't to be mollified.

"Well I'm glad it's only one at a time," he said. "I'm glad *Mr* Sheldrake won't be there."

"Yes, that is lucky," Mrs Fowler agreed.

"That's the second time you've said we're lucky," he complained. "And what's the point of me, when all I come top at is football and metal-work, making friends with a city tycoon who collects antiques and a lady who's fiftieth second cousin to royalty and gives lectures on statues in her spare time. And both of them about ninety, I shouldn't wonder. And Matthew says they can't stand boys."

"Oh, George. It does seem daft. But I thought it

was a job for you and me out of all the family. I thought we could stick up for the poor downtrodden Fowlers of this world."

George had to grin. He'd always appreciated his mother's special brand of humour. Suddenly he didn't feel unhappy or angry any more.

"It's a lot of rot," he agreed. "Dad needs shaking up. He ought to come to our new school. Why doesn't he? It's always you at open day and parent–teacher meetings."

"He's a very shy man."

George shrugged.

"I think he's scared. As if it matters what the other parents are like. We never know what they do or who they are. We don't care. Might be doctors or van drivers or pop stars or mind a printing machine like Dad or on public assistance. If I stay on to take A-levels in the second year sixth–what a hope–I might marry a surprise myself. There's some fantastic girls."

"Not just yet, George, please. Let's settle Polly and the Sheldrakes first."

The bus was a long time coming. Mrs Fowler kept looking up at a clock sticking out of the side of the shop next to the bus stop, and then at a piece of paper in her hand.

"We could take a taxi," George suggested in a lordly way, in the voice he answered Polly with when she started swanking.

Mrs Fowler laughed outright. They both felt more ordinary. The bus came.

"Is it far?" George asked.

"Not very. Odd place, London. Slums in one

street, villas in the next. Same in any big city, I suppose. All changing now, but not fast enough for me. Might as well go inside. Think I remember where we get off." She looked at the piece of paper again. "Polly's given me the instructions."

"Telling us not to wipe our fingers on the table-cloth, I daresay."

"There won't be a tablecloth."

This was more like Mum's normal self.

"You're only guessing," George retorted. "You don't know anything about it. Polly lays it on thick for me and the kids, but she doesn't say much about the Sheldrakes in front of you and Dad. I've noticed that."

"You notice too much. You're like me. You don't just see what's in front of your nose like Dad. We might not be the cleverest ones in the family, George, but we're sensitive to atmosphere."

"I'm nothing of the sort," George protested. "I'm curious. And so are you."

They both started to laugh – more than they usually would at such a feeble attempt to be jolly.

"We'd better calm down," Mrs Fowler said soberly.

"I heard Polly warn you – 'mind you don't get over-excited'. I know what she said – 'you and George are a fine pair'."

"Something like that," Mrs Fowler admitted. "Polly mightn't tell me much except how to behave myself, but I often have a proper chat to Matthew. He's very pleased we're going to see his mother this afternoon."

"Oh is he," George muttered, but then relented.

"Matthew's not bad. Buys smashing presents and that's not always easy, even when money's no object. He chooses exactly what we've been wanting for ages without us telling him. The kids think he's an all-the-year-round Father Christmas."

"He told Mr Fowler, when they first met after the wedding, that he envied him having such a large family and admired the way you were all brought up."

"What on earth did Dad say?"

"Just grunted."

They both laughed again.

"Don't get anywhere flattering Dad. I could have told Matthew that. He looks at you as if you're in the witness box and you stop buttering him up and say what you want straight out. If you've been telling lies, he makes you feel as small as a decimal halfpenny."

"That's no news to me. Polly says Dad ought to be chosen for the Ombudsman."

They were both quiet for a little while, thinking this over. George looked out of the window. It was true what Mrs Fowler had just said about how different next-door parts of London were. Where they lived was very near, but it could be another world that he saw out of the bus now. There were no old tenement buildings, like the one the Fowlers lived in, that were going to be pulled down goodness knows when. George knew his family had been on the waiting list for a new council flat for years. If he'd had some little sisters instead of brothers, the council might have obliged, but they didn't seem to care about five boys sharing a room. There were only two bedrooms – the other one was for Mum and Dad. Polly used to sleep on a couch in the living-room and keep her things in a cupboard in the passage. There was no bathroom – only a place to wash – and the lavatory was out on the landing.

The bus passed a square with grass and trees, where the houses had long windows and arched door-ways and weren't joined on to each other. There were a few modern blocks of flats, but not very big or high, not like the tower estate down by the river that the Fowlers would be moved to when the tenements were at last demolished. George looked around at what seemed like miles of sky and acres of space, at the clean bright shops, the broad pavements, and the swept gutters. He began to have the glimmer of an idea of how Polly had felt about escaping. He hadn't thought about it properly before, because she'd always been a pretty decent big sister, helping with the kids and all that. She'd always been a fusspot, too, making them wipe their noses in the middle of a game. She'd appreciate the change.

"Are they very well off?" he asked, wonderingly, and not in his usual Sheldrake-scoffing voice.

Mrs Fowler was vaguely looking out of the bus window, with Polly's instructions clutched in her hand all the time.

"A stockbroker for stockbrokers," she answered, as if she was making it up as she went along. "I don't really understand." She stood up, sat down, and looked at the piece of paper again. "He just signs his name, Matthew says, and millions of pounds appear out of nowhere and land up in his bank account."

"You sound a bit green," George remarked. "Money is the root of all evil, don't forget."

Mrs Fowler giggled. That was what made Mum

16

such good company. She could always see the funny side of things, even when she was upset or thinking about something else, or even if it was against herself. She could keep it up too.

"As long as we have our health and happiness," she chanted, rolling her eyes up to heaven like the old girl who came in once a week to tell them what their future would be like out in the great big wicked world.

On an ordinary day, they would have carried on acting the fool like this until they dried up, but today Mrs Fowler was serious again almost immediately.

"I don't think Mr Sheldrake could ever be bothered with Matthew – he had a lonely childhood," Mrs Fowler resumed. "No one to play with, and never allowed out of his room without his nurse because of all the precious objects lying around. They thought more of their collection than of their son and heir, he says. Shipped him off to boarding-school before he was seven. But when he married Polly, his mother seemed to wake up to the fact that he'd been neglected and that's why he fell for a warm-hearted home-loving girl."

"Neglected!" George nearly shouted. "His own room and all the toys he wanted, and going to the country every holiday when he wasn't at the seaside or abroad, and choosing his own clothes, and having his own car when he was seventeen ... "

"It's a matter of opinion," Mrs Fowler said sternly. "In some ways you don't know how lucky ... "

"If you say that again, I'm going home," George threatened.

"I didn't mean about Mrs Sheldrake asking us to tea. I meant ... "

"I know what you meant," George said. "What's the matter with you, Mum? You know I always know what you're getting at. You don't have to spell it out."

"Sorry, George. There are times though when I feel downright angry with those Sheldrakes. Bringing up a *boy* like that. If there's one thing I know something about it's boys. Guess what Matthew told me once?"

"Once!" George was scathing. "He seems to have told you his life history about ninety-nine hundred times."

George had a queer feeling in his chest while he said this, and Mrs Fowler put out her hand as if she might touch him. They both knew he was jealous.

"Anyway, I'm no good at guessing," he said quickly, "and whatever Matthew told you, I don't think millionaires ought to keep on grumbling."

"If there's anyone who's keeping on grumbling," Mrs Fowler began, but then she stopped. If this outing was going to lead to a quarrel between her and George then she'd rather go home too. She looked at Polly's instructions again instead of looking at George, then leaped to her feet and pulled the bellcord over their head two or three times.

"Here we are," she cried. "Nearly missed it."

Two

"Just in time," she panted, as they jumped down at the request stop and the bus continued along the main road at some speed. Her piece of paper was very crumpled by now. She smoothed it out. First left, second right. Number eleven. First left was a crescent. There were trees growing along the kerb at regular intervals. Some of the houses had gardens and drives and fences, like the country. The biggest houses, George observed, had several push-button bells next to the door: that meant they were divided into flats. Not so grand after all. Second right out of the crescent was a wide, quiet road. All the front doors were painted a different colour. There was very little traffic about and the houses had garages, so you could see the shape of the road without rows of cars lining the middle and edges of it. Hardly any of the houses had television aerials, or you couldn't see them. It made the roofs look good.

"Nice isn't it?" Mrs Fowler said wistfully. George couldn't help agreeing.

Number eleven had four steps and a sort of marble path to the front door. At each side of the steps was a stone pillar with a stone urn on top, carved with animals and filled with moss and flowers. The knocker on the front door was a silver dolphin, sideways on, with one sparkling eye.

"I suppose that's a diamond," George said, but he

didn't feel very sarcastic. It didn't seem like London at all. It didn't seem like the 1970s. You could hardly believe in moon rockets or cholera plagues, standing on the Sheldrakes' doorstep. When the door was opened by a maid in uniform, George thought for one awful moment that he had been transported back in time to the early Victorians they were having lessons on now. Not his favourite subject.

The way the maid eyed him up and down brought him to his senses.

"Sheldrake," he announced brazenly. "Which floor?"

"Oh, George," his mother whispered, "it's all theirs. The whole house. Not flats."

She smiled at the maid who did not change her expression of polite disapproval.

"Mrs Sheldrake is expecting us," Mrs Fowler said, trying to be as haughty as the maid. George could have kicked himself. Instead he kicked the bottom of the door. The maid shuddered and Mrs Fowler frowned. They went in.

They followed the maid through a hall and up some stairs that curved round the hall and had wrought-iron banisters like park railings. There was furniture everywhere, and carpets hanging on the walls as well as umpteen dozen mirrors with heavy frames much larger than the looking-glass inside. There was an enormous chandelier in the hall made from different kinds of pink crystal shapes – globes, spheres, cy-linders, cubes and pyramids – that distantly and musically vibrated. George could hardly take his eyes and ears off it and nearly fell down the stairs looking backwards. The maid flung open two white doors that met in the middle and Mrs Sheldrake rose to greet them from a velvet chair with a gold eagle sticking up from the top of it.

The whole room was crowded with little tables covered with what looked to George like the contents of several antique shops. There were some cupboards with glass fronts full of sculptured heads and painted plates and that sort of thing, and you couldn't see the walls for pictures. George was worried about moving forwards to shake hands with Mrs Sheldrake (Polly's instructions again): he was sure he'd fall over something. Mum had been dead right not to bring the kids. It was like a visit to a museum and George had always excused himself from that kind of school outing. Mrs Sheldrake started on a long stream of gush, the minute they were all sitting down. George was surprised any of the furniture was to use. He balanced on the edge of his chair – another velvet one but with a gold owl on top. There was a whole set of them. Mrs Fowler's chair had some bird George couldn't recognize. He didn't listen to what Mrs Sheldrake was saying.

Mrs Fowler wasn't listening either. She was gazing round as if she was in the *Arabian Nights*. It didn't matter because Mrs Sheldrake didn't give them a chance to speak. George stared round, too, but not in the same struck-dumb way as Mum. More as if he'd seen it all before. At least he couldn't complain that there wasn't anything to look at. There was no sign of any tea.

"George!"

Mrs Sheldrake suddenly called out his name like his form master, and he almost stood to attention and

21

said "yes, sir". Fortunately she went on talking.

"Polly tells me you're good at metal-work. I expect you admired the balustrade?"

George nodded knowingly, but once more thankful that Mrs Sheldrake didn't pause for replies.

"Mr Sheldrake has a very fine collection of weapons worked in silver and steel," she continued. "I'll show them to you later on. They're in that ebony and rose-wood showcase over there."

George thought that might be really worth coming for, but "later on" was ominous. Sounded as if they would be there half the night. He wished his mother would act more like herself and stop saying "really beautiful" and "ever so pretty", and that Mrs Sheldrake would stop handing her all the objects off the little tables to gape at. They'd never get any tea at this rate, especially as Mrs Sheldrake kept on explaining the history of everything. George felt smothered by his ignorance, as if she was pulling a sack over his head. Now they were starting off on the family! He wondered whether he dared to prowl round the room or to say out loud that he was hungry.

"Six altogether, isn't it? Polly and George and Thomas and Sidney and then Philip and Henry. They'd give you a medal in Russia for glorious motherhood, Mrs Fowler. It must be a struggle, but then there are all these family allowances nowadays."

"It's not so much the money. Those allowances don't keep five growing boys in shoe leather. Mr Fowler's always had a steady job. It's keeping an eye on everything all at once. Polly's been a help."

"I expect you were as cross as we were at not being

consulted about the wedding until it was all over. It makes things a little difficult between us, but I'm sure we can cope."

"It is a bit awkward," Mrs Fowler agreed.

"Our stupid husbands have such outdated ideas," Mrs Sheldrake began again, but with one eye on George who was scraping his feet on the rung of his chair that was made of plaited wood. "Mr Sheldrake still believes that money should marry money and he did have the perfect wife in mind for Matthew, so naturally he was disappointed. I think Polly's a sweet girl myself."

After this there was a long silence, until George decided it was time to ask for tea, whether he was hungry or not. Mrs Sheldrake rang a bell for the maid, who popped into the room immediately, like a genie out of a bottle, with a trolley. George was relieved when he saw that there were sandwiches. Very small, thin sandwiches with the crusts cut off, but plenty of stuffing inside. No cake, but a plateful of chocolate biscuits. The plate was made of such delicate china you could see through it, and Mrs Fowler held on to it tightly with both hands while she passed it to George. The cups had frilled edges and no handles and were made of pleated china, and the tea was as pale as straw and tasted like it. Mrs Sheldrake wasn't hungry and Mrs Fowler kept nibbling at the same biscuit. George ate the whole plateful of sandwiches and then started on the rest of the biscuits, ignoring his mother's prods.

"I suppose", Mrs Fowler said desperately, trying to distract Mrs Sheldrake's attention from George making a pig of himself, "that if Mr Sheldrake felt so badly about Polly and Matthew it was very good of him to set them up in that nice house."

Polly and Matthew lived in a crummy-looking joint about five centuries old near Richmond Park: inside was all right though, with an attic converted into what Polly called "creative space" and a basement made into a games room with a billiard-table and darts and skittles. George often went there. Matthew let the kids rampage wherever they liked, but Polly kept telling them "don't", as if she'd never married and left home at all. George came out of his reverie to find there was another long embarrassed silence. Then Mrs Sheldrake said,

"As a matter of fact, Mr Sheldrake didn't do anything for them. They're such an independent pair."

George and Mrs Fowler were surprised. All the Fowlers had taken it for granted that Matthew's parents had handed over a large cheque. That was one of his worries Dad didn't let them forget. If he'd been told in advance, at least he could have done his duty and provided a white wedding with a feast afterwards. That's what he was always on about. Perhaps when he heard that Mr Sheldrake hadn't given Polly and Matthew a sack of gold he'd stop nagging. George was amazed when Mrs Fowler continued the conversation. Usually she told Dad not to brood.

"That's odd," she said. "They surely hadn't saved up enough themselves."

"Good heavens no, not in that short time. They had known each other for less than six months, so I'm told. Altogether too hasty."

"Love at first sight," Mrs Fowler replied, and George had to stuff several biscuits into his mouth at once to stop snorting. Mrs Sheldrake didn't seem to understand Mum was making one of her dry remarks.

"If you believe in that sort of nonsense," she said sharply. "I should think marry in haste repent at leisure would be more applicable. Such an extraordinary way they met, too. On one of those organized walks for some charity or other."

"That's right," George interrupted. "For Shelter. Polly's mad keen on all that. Helps at the Youth Club and visited all the old ladies in the buildings for Task Force, when she was in the sixth form. She makes Matthew take some of them out for a ride in his car on Sundays."

"Does she?" Mrs Sheldrake was astounded.

"She can make Matthew do anything," George added, not caring if he was tactless. He wasn't prepared to be on his best behaviour for someone who purposely made his mother miserable, not for a hundred Matthews.

"Then I suppose it was Polly's idea", Mrs Sheldrake asked pointedly, "to sell the picture Matthew's godmother gave him when he was twenty-one, in order to buy the house and furnish it, without asking any favours of us?"

Mrs Fowler looked blank.

"First I've heard of it," she said. She and George looked at each other. They knew they were thinking the same thing. *One* picture enough to buy a house and everything you wanted to put in it! They hardly heard what Mrs Sheldrake was saying they were so stupefied.

"It was the best picture she had. Matthew was her favourite godson. Mr Sheldrake was furious when he heard that Matthew had sold it. Would have been worth fifty thousand in five years, if he'd hung on to it. Values are increasing all the time."

She might as well have been talking to herself. George and Mrs Fowler were busy counting the pictures. There were about fifty on the wall facing George. All he had to do was take *one* down, tuck it under his arm, and march off with it. George wasn't quite sure whether Mrs Fowler was thinking the same as him about that. She'd never do such a thing, but, sitting there on the velvet chair surrounded by enough marvels for a whole exhibition, George thought he might. They surely wouldn't miss *one* out of so many. The idea slid into his mind. It did more than that. It took hold of him completely. He didn't resist either. He was bored stiff with all this chat about Polly and Matthew. He let the idea gain possession, gave himself up to it. He didn't necessarily have to take a picture – something small enough to put in his pocket would be more sensible, as long as it was worth a fortune. How would he sell what he took? He'd think of a way. He began to feel proud of his idea and not in the least ashamed.

Then he quite suddenly remembered what Matthew had told him about the only two things he had enjoyed doing with his mother and father. They let him help with the catalogue. Every tiny object was listed in it, together with a description, its history, its value, and where it was insured and for how much, and in which exhibitions it had appeared all over the world. There was one copy of the catalogue deposited with Mr Sheldrake's bank manager and another with his solicitors. Even the smallest article would be missed. Nothing was left out of the catalogue, Matthew had said, not even the miniature silver thimble with the initials of some famous character engraved on it. George forgot who it was that Matthew had said – a historical personage probably. George wasn't very good at history. Now that this special idea had entered his head, he began to wish he was. It would be important to know something about the Sheldrake collection. That would be the first step. George was amazed at how fast his mind was running on, as if he'd been thinking about this idea and how to by-pass the catalogue for weeks, instead of this very afternoon. He didn't want to run the risk of stealing something and then find out it wasn't worth very much. Anything from ten pounds to ten thousand, Matthew had said.

There was the second thing – the burglar alarm. Matthew had told him that all the most valuable items were connected up on some electric circuit to a gigantic police whistle outside the front door which all the local policemen knew about. Matthew had liked the job of having to set the alarm when they went away on holiday. There were grilles and padlocks on the ground floor windows and several Chubb locks on the front door too, but that wouldn't affect George. He'd make his attempt from inside the house of course. He'd be already there – invited again. He ought to start being polite from now, if he wanted that to happen. He'd ask for another cup of that peculiar tea, as there wasn't anything left to eat. There was no need. They hadn't noticed he'd been miles away. His mother and Mrs Sheldrake were still pretending to have a polite conversation themselves.

27

He'd make the kids die of laughing with an imitation. Have to wait until Dad wasn't around though. Wonder what Dad would say about all this. That was something George would rather not dwell on.

"Polly tells me you're moving to a modern flat soon," Mrs Sheldrake was saying.

"This year next year sometime never," Mrs Fowler replied.

"I should grow tired of waiting too," Mrs Sheldrake agreed, as if she knew all about tenements being pulled down, and housing lists. "Why do you stay in the centre of town? I'm sure there are some quite cheap houses to be had on the outskirts. You don't have to rely on the council, do you?"

"I don't have a rich godmother," Mrs Fowler said, and this time Mrs Sheldrake actually saw the joke. She smiled in a sickly way.

"One wouldn't be able to amass much capital with six children to bring up, I do appreciate that, but ... "

"Is amassing capital the same as saving up?" George asked.

"Not exactly," Mrs Sheldrake said coldly, not bothering to make explanations to a boy who was scraping his feet on the rung of her exquisite chair. She kept glaring at him, but George kept forgetting.

"It isn't only the money," Mrs Fowler began again, in an apologetic voice.

"You've said that once already." George was angry with his mother for making excuses. They were supposed to be sticking up for themselves, weren't they? Mrs Sheldrake gave him a disgusted look, as if to say what a rude, badly brought up child. George didn't care about her, but he did wish he hadn't been insolent when Mrs Fowler suddenly looked as if she might burst into tears. George had never seen her look like that before.

"It's Mr Fowler," she continued. "He's often on the night shift and I wouldn't like to think of him having a long journey home on top of it. We're only five stations on the tube where we are now."

"I imagine it could be tiring, without a car."

George thought he might say something even ruder if Mrs Sheldrake didn't shut up. All she had to do was take a picture off the wall and say "have this", if she was really sorry for them. Not that George would have liked it, if his mother had accepted. He'd rather steal one. The idea crept back into his head again. George feared it had come to stay.

Three

"What about those weapons?" George asked, trying not to sound as surly as he felt.

"Of course. How dreary for you – sitting there listening to us. Enough to make any barbarian of a schoolboy scrape his feet."

George and his mother exchanged a brief glance of commiseration, while Mrs Sheldrake rang for the maid to wheel the trolley away. She crossed the room again and beckoned them to follow her to a big cupboard. It was made of red and black wood in interlocking sections, and each section was squared off with a mother-of-pearl frame. There was no glass in front like the others. Mrs Sheldrake unlocked it with an enormous key big enough to open the Tower of London. The key was kept in a hollowed-out segment on the top of the cupboard, with a little wooden shutter for a lid that folded itself back into the thick framework.

"That's a neat job," George commented.

"Ah, they knew how to make things in those days," Mrs Sheldrake replied, as she fitted the key into the lock.

When the doors were drawn back to their fullest extent, a light came on and showed up the inside.

"That's clever," George said to his mother, who was standing beside him.

The sides and top and bottom of the cupboard were lined with dark green silky velvet stuff. There were shelves across the whole width and each one was narrower than the one below, like steps. The topmost very narrow shelf seemed to be empty, but the light didn't shine up there or into the corners. The other shelves were laid out with knives and spearheads and very old pistols and swords and sabres, all gleaming against the dark soft background. Mrs Sheldrake took one or two out and let George hold them.

"They're all in working order, even the most ancient," she said. "Beautifully preserved. Be careful of the knives. They're sharp."

George looked at everything very thoroughly and handed everything back very carefully. It was tantalizing just looking at things you'd really like to use – that was the trouble with museums.

Mrs Sheldrake was about to close the cupboard, when George tripped on the fringe of an embroidered cloth draped over the nearest little table. He put out his hand to stop himself falling head first among the knives and pistols, and grabbed hold of the top narrow shelf, remembering that it was empty. He regained his balance, but the shelf tipped down and he heard something rattle. Mrs Sheldrake began to close the cupboard doors, but George held on to her arm without thinking. She looked down at his hand clutching on to her and George quickly pulled it away.

"What's that up there?" he asked abruptly. "Right at the back in the middle." He stood on his toes, holding on to his mother this time, and leaned forward. "It's hideous!" he exclaimed, shrinking away and stepping back on Mrs Fowler.

"George!" she said reprovingly, and not because he had hurt her toes.

Mrs Sheldrake gave an artificial laugh.

31

"Quite a critic. Not many people are brave enough to admit that works of art can be ugly. Especially to the owner's face."

She looked rather reluctantly into the cupboard.

"It's my husband's special pride and joy. I'm afraid I can't let you near it – I'm not allowed to touch it myself. Not that I ever want to."

"Couldn't I just see it properly," George persisted.

Mrs Sheldrake sighed. Mrs Fowler slightly shook her head at George but he pretended he hadn't seen her. He looked eagerly and expectantly at Mrs Sheldrake.

"There is another light here. Usually I have to ask Mr Sheldrake's permission to switch on. He's rather secretive on this subject. Don't ask me why. However," she continued doubtfully, "I suppose in the circumstances … "

"I didn't exactly mean ugly," George said, thinking Mrs Sheldrake was annoyed with him for saying something bad about their treasures. "I meant more like a creature in a nightmare. I mean I wasn't afraid."

His mother looked at him in bewilderment, but Mrs Sheldrake nodded.

"I know exactly what you meant," she said, sounding human for the first time for the whole afternoon. "There's something nasty about it. I often think so. I hate it."

They were all silent. Suddenly she switched on another light.

"There!" she said. "It's ridiculous to be so superstitious, simply because Mr Sheldrake is so peculiarly possessive about it. We don't even list it in the catalogue. He never lends it for an exhibition."

The thought that it might not be connected to the alarm if it wasn't in the catalogue flitted through George's mind, though he had stopped thinking about his wicked idea while he was looking at the weapons.

"I suppose if no one knows he's got it," George suggested, "then they won't ask him to lend it to put on show. So he doesn't need to make a record of it."

"He has shown it privately, from time to time, to a few intimate friends," Mrs Sheldrake replied. "I've no idea why it's left out of the catalogue. And as for wanting any record of it – not if Mr Sheldrake can help it. He's never let anyone else touch it."

"Any drawings?" George asked.

"Not since it's been in Mr Sheldrake's possession. There may be some old ones – possibly in an encyclopaedia somewhere."

"What about photographs?" George asked. He spoke naturally and familiarly, as if he was having a conversation with his mother. She was standing there thunderstruck. Mrs Sheldrake had stopped being catty too. As if they were on the same side at last, against the object in the cupboard. George half-felt he didn't want to look at it now, but the other half of him was strangely excited.

It was displayed in the glare of a very bright spotlight that made George and Mrs Fowler blink, but Mrs Sheldrake was suddenly occupied in rearranging the fringed cloth on the table. The hideous object dazzled their eyes. It was small enough to hold in your hand, or put in your pocket, but every detail stood out. George didn't know why it made him shudder, but he was sure that the evil look in its flashing eyes would make you turn your back, like

Mrs Sheldrake, if you had seen it before. Mrs Fowler wasn't particularly impressed either way, but there were some things they didn't agree on. She'd never go into the snake house at the Zoo for instance. She asked if she could help Mrs Sheldrake put the things straight on the table that George had tripped against. They left him to gaze into the cupboard alone, although George sensed that Mrs Sheldrake was keeping an eye on him.

He examined it scientifically, concentrating on the details. That was the way to deal with superstition. It had the head of a man, grinning, with rows of teeth, and the body of a wild beast. It had a remarkable tail, with spikes shooting out all the way along, and the end of each spike was tipped with a sparkling gem. Although it was small, it had a massive look and feel to it. George supposed it was solid gold all through and he wondered how heavy it would be to hold, or to carry about in his pocket. He was sure the sparkling gems at the end of each spike must be precious stones – rubies, emeralds, sapphires and that sort of thing. Even that wouldn't make it worth thousands of pounds, unless it was incredibly old or unique, or made by some genius. George wanted to ask Mrs Sheldrake dozens of questions, but something stopped him showing any more curiosity, except to say,

"What's it called?"

"A manticora," Mrs Sheldrake replied, as if there were hundreds of them. She switched off the spotlight, tipped the shelf level again, closed the doors, locked the cupboard, put back the key, and covered it with the shutter. None of them said anything else about it and Mrs Sheldrake looked at her watch when

George and his mother prepared to sit down again. George knew the truce was over.

"Time we were going," Mrs Fowler said. "We've had such a lovely afternoon. So interesting."

That wasn't what Polly had told George to say.

"Thank you for having me," he recited, feeling like one of the kids taking a balloon home from a bun-fight.

"Not at all," Mrs Sheldrake replied. "Do come again."

"I'd like to," George said at once, thinking of the Manticora, but Mrs Sheldrake wasn't too delighted with this reply and his mother gave him a prod. Mrs Sheldrake rang for the maid to show them out.

"You won't mind if I don't come down," she told, rather than asked, them. "I must meet my husband fairly soon – a business dinner."

When Mrs Fowler and George were ushered out and the door closed behind them, it was almost lighting-up time. They started to walk to the bus stop, without saying anything. The road was tranquil in the dusk and there was a fragrant earthy smell from the gardens. The air was a deep blue colour and the first star came out. George again had the sensation of time going backwards, or at any rate standing still. He almost wished they could stay in the street a little while, instead of hurrying back to their mingy tene-ment flat in the dingy block where the dirty street was scattered all over with litter. His mother wasn't look-ing at him at all. She had her face sideways and seemed to be watching the front doors go by like a film. Or else she had a stiff neck.

"Anything wrong?" George asked.

35

"Mrs Sheldrake can come and visit us next time," she mumbled.

"There won't be a next time," George said. "She nearly had a fit when I said I wanted to come again."

"So did I." Mrs Fowler spoke in a muffled voice, not turning her head and not sounding as if she was even smiling.

"I didn't like it all that much," George added hastily. He didn't want to mention the Manticora to his mother. He didn't know why. Yes he did. The Manticora had become the centrepiece of his idea. He wanted to concentrate all his thoughts on it, but at the same time he wished he could forget he'd ever seen it. If there was one person he could talk to about things that vaguely bothered him it was his mother, but he wanted to keep the Manticora and his idea to himself. Later on perhaps, when his plans were advanced ... "It just made a change, that's all," he said, trying to sound distant. His mother didn't reply. George thought she must be annoyed because he had been enthusiastic about going again. In the same way that he was annoyed because she kept on about Matthew. "I certainly didn't like *her*," he said firmly.

Mrs Fowler made a queer noise in her throat, a gulping noise. Then she said,

"Don't be too hard on her, George. She's used to people who think having a chat is scoring points off each other all the time."

"She certainly scored some off us," George agreed. "I wish I'd scraped my feet a jolly sight harder on her mouldy old chair. I'm not going to be sorry for her while she's sitting up there in the lap of luxury with maids rushing in and out with trolleys."

"It was a lovely place wasn't it?" Mrs Fowler said. "It's no use our pretending we weren't impressed, George. We were both carried away."

Now George didn't answer. He daren't admit how far he had been carried away. He knew at that moment that the idea would never be shaken off now. He had the same feeling again that had engulfed him when Mrs Sheldrake had told them about Matthew's god-mother and the picture. If one picture was enough to buy Polly and Matthew's house and fill it up with furniture, then surely the Manticora would be just what he wanted for his idea. Small enough to carry away in his pocket. Not in the catalogue. All by itself on that dark shelf and hardly ever shown to anyone. They wouldn't miss it for ages and then it would be too late. He was suddenly conscious that his mother was staring at him. He looked back at her, still think-ing of the Manticora. He saw a tear slide down her cheek and plop on her hand. She didn't wipe it away. He was petrified. He'd never once seen his mother cry.

"Don't take any notice," she said. "It's envy. That's a bad feeling. I ought to be ashamed."

"Of course I'm going to take some notice," George told her angrily. "I'll do a lot more than take notice. You'll see."

Mrs Fowler tried to laugh.

"Sounds as if you're going to fight the dragon," she said.

Or the Manticora, George thought, and then he called himself a fool. His idea was more like a fairy story than a practical plan. He would make it come true, though. He wouldn't be found out. He wasn't going to stand Mrs Sheldrake making his mother cry. Or his mother having to manage in their cramped and dismal flat while *one* picture would buy ... George shook his head violently, but the wicked thoughts went on raging inside.

"I'm serious," he said grandly to his mother. "If I do something about raising enough cash to buy *us* a house, will you promise to agree to everything I tell you from now on, and not to ask any questions?"

"Such as?" Mrs Fowler was cynical.

"Such as where I've suddenly discovered fifteen thousand pounds," George replied, very solemnly.

"Only if you've robbed a bank, you mean, not which one?"

Now it was George's turn to try to laugh.

"Don't fret, George," Mrs Fowler said. "It'll pass off. A moment's weakness, that's all. Forget it. Here's the bus."

"Let's walk home, Mum. We'll feel more like ourselves again by then. We don't want Dad and Polly to think Mrs Sheldrake's been one too many for us."

"Right as usual, George. We'd better step it out. I promised we'd be back by the time Matthew came to collect Polly, and we stayed longer than I meant. I didn't want to drag you away from those old guns – the only treat of the afternoon for you."

George didn't remind his mother of the Manticora in the same cupboard. She obviously hadn't registered what a deep impression it had made on him, which was all to the good.

"We'll stick to the main road," she said. "We don't want to lose our way."

Four

They walked on, both deep in their own thoughts, as they had been when they started out.

"I suppose fifteen thousand pounds would be enough?" George said suddenly.

Mrs Fowler laughed helplessly.

"Enough for a castle," she said, and added, "in the air."

"It's not a joke," George warned her. "You'll see. How much would a house cost?"

"A mansion like the Sheldrakes'?" Mrs Fowler teased him.

"Of course not," he replied impatiently. "One to suit us. We don't want a palace full of old junk. Would ten thousand cover everything?"

Mrs Fowler gave George a sidelong glance and stopped laughing.

"Yes," she told him. Then all at once she was enthusiastic, not simply humouring him. George listened while she gabbled on, rather like Mrs Sheldrake when they had arrived, not giving herself time to breathe.

"It would cost twelve thousand pounds where we'd want it to be – not right out in one of those new towns, but in an old-fashioned suburb with character. I wouldn't want a new house either, nor a historic monument like Polly and Matthew's. It would be one of those desirable Victorian family residences, George, but without a basement. I don't like basements. Lots of space and a rundown garden the kids could do what they liked in. With a tree. They could have a swing. In front I'd have a row of bushes and a low wall. Nice to be private for a change."

Mrs Fowler was staring ahead as if the actual house was growing out of the pavement before their eyes.

"You go through a gate and up a short path with black and white diamond-shaped tiles. The front door's inside a glass porch big enough to keep a few pot plants in. Open the door and there's a hall, a proper part of the house, not just a gloryhole where you boys can chuck your belongings the minute you're inside. A large front room for best – Christmas and parties and Sundays – and at the back an enormous kitchen where we'd spend most of the time. There's French doors leading out of it on to the garden and, through an arch in the wall, there's a small room we could eat in, if anyone posh enough came who wouldn't want to eat in the kitchen itself."

"Mrs Sheldrake," George suggested.

His mother didn't hear. She went on as if she was talking in her sleep.

"Upstairs on the first floor would be a big bedroom for me and your father, and another one for Phil and Henry, and the bathroom. There'd be showers and handbasins and separate lavatories as well as this bathroom, masses of hot water, airing cupboards, immersion heaters. We'd have to take the old boiler out and the kitchen range."

"That would be another thousand on the bill," George said. "Plumbing's expensive."

Mrs Fowler merely nodded and rushed on.

"The next floor would have three rooms, too. One for Tom and Sid. One for you, George. And a spare room if anyone wanted to stay."

"Matthew and Polly?"

It was no good. Mrs Fowler was deaf.

"And then right up at the top some box-rooms where we could store all our old rubbish instead of having to stuff it all into odd corners where we haven't got room to turn round."

"And the furniture?" George said loudly, so that Mrs Fowler actually stopped for a minute. "I'd want some really modern design. Not ordinary chairs. Leather circles on steel pivots. That kind of thing. And you'd all have to knock on the door of my room before you came in."

"Anything you like if we had fifteen thousand," Mrs Fowler allowed grandly. "Not for me though. I shouldn't want carved woodwork and velvet either. I'd have … "

A glazed look came into Mrs Fowler's eyes and George quickly interrupted her again.

"And you're perfectly sure that it could all come out of fifteen thousand pounds, down to the last egg-cup?"

"Easily," Mrs Fowler said, as if she had the money in her handbag then and there. "Legal fees would run away with a few hundred, and I'd like a second-hand car for Dad for the journey. There is a garage. I mean there would be. In this dream house. If not, it could be a workshop."

"Would it be greedy to think of a car?" George asked.

"Not if it was a very old one," Mrs Fowler decided.

"I don't want us to be greedy," George said.

"Of course not," Mrs Fowler agreed at once.

"I just want us to have what we need. What other people take for granted in this day and age."

"Precisely," Mrs Fowler said. Then she burst out laughing. "We are a pair of idiots, George, playing make-believe like this. Worse than the time we discussed where we would go for a holiday in our private yacht. Good thing we're nearly home – that'll bring us down to earth with a bang."

They turned off the main road into the narrow street lined with tall tenement buildings. One side of it was used as a permanent lorry park.

"At least we can be grateful we don't live on the ground floor," Mrs Fowler said. "They can't ever see the daylight, such as it is, with those great things in front of their windows, week in, week out."

"No sign of Matthew's car," George remarked, looking up and down the street.

"That's a blessing. I hate to be late when they're so obliging."

George and his mother entered the yard and began to climb the outside stone stairs up to their flat. The communal dustbins stank even worse than usual. Some of them were overflowing. Lines of grey washing flapped over the back doors, and there was a confused colossal blare of shouting and telly programmes. A hooter sounded through the din from outside.

"That's Matthew."

They both went back to the street.

"Hallo you two. Bet you're starved. I know what my mother's notion of tea is."

"Are you coming up," Mrs Fowler asked, "or shall I send Polly down?"

"I'll come up of course. Say good night to Henry. I've got a little something for him to celebrate his very first half-term holiday."

Matthew parked his Mini Cooper between two lorries and they all tramped up the stairs, Mrs Fowler in front and George and Matthew close behind. The stairs were damp, dark, smelly and echoing. The walls were scratched all over with names and drawings, and there were piles of dirt and screwed-up paper in all the corners. Matthew hadn't ever noticed. He didn't care if he used a chipped cup without a saucer, sitting at the table covered in the remains of the kids' tea. He didn't care if they came to see him at Richmond with dirty faces and holes in their socks and their clothes torn and their shirts hanging out. Yet he was good at knowing what went on *inside* people. That's how he guessed about presents, and understood when not to bother Mr Fowler, and when to stop Polly criticizing and ordering about. George had asked Matthew about it once.

"You could call it reaction, I suppose," he had said, and that was all. George hadn't properly understood then, but now he had been to Matthew's home he did.

"I must be having what you could call an opposite reaction," George thought to himself, as they trudged up the stairs and all the time he was remembering the pink crystal chandelier and the mirrors, going up the curved staircase at the Sheldrakes.

"You're very subdued," Matthew said to him quietly. "I always feel like that when I've been to see my parents, but I didn't expect it of you, George."

43

"I'm all right. Just thinking. I'd like to know more about all that stuff your mother showed us. I felt a dope not having a clue about anything."

Mrs Fowler came to a stop a few stairs above.

"George!" she exclaimed. "You old hypocrite. You said it was a load of junk on the way home."

"That was just the *furniture*," George began, but Matthew let out a great bellow of laughter.

"If only they could hear you," he said, but was immediately serious when he saw the expression on George's face under the landing light they passed. "I don't see why not," he began again. "It all comes out of books. I'll give you a few to start you off and then you can decide what you're most interested in and borrow some specialist books out of the library. If you're going to do it at all, we might as well tackle the enterprise thoroughly."

George knew there would be nothing about the Manticora in the sort of beginners book Matthew meant. They had art books like that at school. All the usual pictures of the marvels of Italy and Greece and Stonehenge and the Pyramids.

"I can't learn out of books," he said.

"Nor can I," Matthew replied. "That's why I'm an engineer. Broke mother's heart I believe. I was meant to be an art historian."

Art and history! George's two worst things. They tried to make out at school that what he did for the metal-work competitions was artistic, but George knew better. It was more like engineering. But he'd have to work at art and history if he was to be sure of the fifteen thousand pounds. It wouldn't be a crime at all. It would be a sacrifice. He'd be a saint, not a thief.

44

Saying the word to himself made George waver for a second, but the single tear that Mrs Fowler had shed on the way home was something George would never forget. He must go on picking Matthew's brains, even if the answer wasn't what he wanted or expected. It was his only chance. How else was he to find out what he wanted to know quickly.

"I don't exactly want to start from the beginning," he explained cautiously. "I'm better at learning about what I've actually seen. I'd like to explore further on the subject of the things your mother actually showed us this afternoon."

"All those old guns," Mrs Fowler called down from half a flight of stairs ahead. "You could go to the Tower of London again – they've got roomfuls of them."

"Not only those," George said very quietly to Matthew, waiting for Mrs Fowler to climb out of earshot. "There were some small figures of wild animals and ... "

"I used to like those," Matthew admitted. "I took one off its table once and put it on my bedroom shelf. There was hell to pay." He paused reflectively. George dreaded he would start off on one of those childhood reminiscences Mrs Fowler had quoted.

"What can I do if I don't like reading?" George asked abruptly.

"The practical approach," Matthew instantly replied. "I'm all for it myself. Enough of this mooning. You could do worse than go to some of Mother's lectures. She always talks about something in the collection, so she can take some examples to arouse envy and covetousness in the audience."

George knew Mrs Sheldrake wouldn't be taking the Manticora anywhere, but he'd let himself in for it now.

"Where at?" he asked.

"The Poly, London University, Goldsmiths', Westminster Tech – take your choice. They start in September, so you won't have missed many. I'll send you her timetable and you can choose whichever strikes a chord. I imagine you'd be most interested in the bronzes. Otherwise it's all china and glass and furniture. Dreary."

"Do you have to have a ticket?"

"No. Just walk in. Free for all who come, which isn't many as a rule."

They'd reached the top landing. Mrs Fowler had gone in and left the door open for them.

"Don't *send* anything," George begged. "They'd only laugh at me, and Dad would think I'd gone over to the enemy. Don't say anything will you?"

Matthew crossed his heart and promised.

"I'll think of some other way of letting you know."

"Not even to Polly," George insisted, as she rushed out of the flat on to the landing where they were talking.

"Don't come in," she said to Matthew. "Dad's standing on his dignity. 'Nothing but treachery whichever way I turn.' It would be funny if it weren't so infuriating."

She was trying to sound amused and uncaring, but George could tell she was cross. Matthew was distressed.

"Oh dear. How I wish … "

He stopped and looked quickly at George.

"Never mind. Just as you say, Polly. You know best. Give this parcel to Henry, will you, George? I'm sorry I shall miss seeing him open it. Remember that swinging magnet toy he was so entranced with in the shop window near the station, last time you came to Richmond for the day?"

"He'll go crazy," George said, taking the parcel.

"Oh, Matthew," Polly moaned. "I'm sorry, and when you're so ... "

Matthew shook his head and this time Polly looked at George as if she'd never seen him properly before.

"I suppose", George said to them, as they stood there together on the dark landing, "if you'd asked Dad's permission to get married you'd have had to wait until you were both a hundred years old. And, after this afternoon, I can see why Mr Sheldrake ... "

"Don't *you* start worrying about the family feud," Matthew interrupted swiftly. "And, as far as this afternoon's concerned, you've done your noble bit. It'll all come right if we leave it to time the great healer. Good night now."

They clattered down the stone stairs, taking them three at once. They were already laughing and happy by the time they reached the last landing before the street. George could hear them. He went indoors with the parcel for Henry. He didn't feel very happy himself. He felt as if he were two boys. One George was guilty and ashamed at what Matthew would think of his Manticora idea, and the other George was absolutely set on helping Mum out of this pigsty. It was all very well for Polly and Matthew to laugh. They weren't forced to spend the rest of the evening with Dad laying down the law and nowhere else to go except the tiny bedroom, where there'd be a scarf hung over the light to cast a shade, so that Phil and Henry could get to sleep while Tom and Sid did their homework. The kids wouldn't want to stay in the living-room with Mum and Dad, any more than he would, if there was going to be one of those terrible arguments about the Sheldrakes.

George decided he didn't like half-term much. Or ordinary holidays either, come to that, cooped up in the yard minding Phil and Henry, except for one week when they hired a caravan at the seaside, and that was even more everyone on top of everyone else. In term-time he could stay late at school as often as he liked – usually in the metal-work studio, if there wasn't any football. Not many people were keen on metal-work. He usually had the place to himself for an hour until the school caretaker came to lock up. George imagined his own room in the house Mrs Fowler had described on the way home – make-believe was just about it.

When he went to bed himself and closed his eyes, George began to wish he hadn't given his idea a name. Wasn't there anything else he could purloin from all that collection? Somehow he knew there wasn't. The Manticora was perfect for his purpose. Small. Not listed. In a cabinet he could persuade Mrs Sheldrake to show him again, if he pretended he was dedicated to guns and knives. But that would be after he had found out how much it was worth. And if it was worth enough, and after he had stolen it, he would have to find a way of disposing of it. He might have to talk to Mum then. Not before. Until then, it was up to him. George wasn't frightened, not until he

48

closed his eyes and there was the Manticora, alive, sitting on the end of the bed, its grinning rows of teeth opening and shutting as if to devour him. He could hear it snarling – a cross between a lion's roar and a wolf's howl. He opened his eyes quickly. It vanished. For once in his life he was glad he was sharing the big bed with Tom and Sid and that Phil and Henry were in their bunks by the window.

Five

George didn't dream about the Manticora again, and Mrs Fowler didn't refer to the visit at all. Mr Fowler kept on saying "I'm the head of this family and you'll all do as I tell you and not go sneaking off behind my back", until something happened at work to upset him and he complained about that instead. George was relieved that his parents seemed to have forgotten all about the visit, but he was surprised that Matthew took no more notice of their conversation on the stairs. The next time they all went to Richmond for the day, a Saturday, George decided he wouldn't mention it, unless Matthew did. He was in two minds again – one half of his brain being glad that everyone was forgetting and the other half pondering on the Manticora.

He took all the kids with him as usual and, while they were all in the attic messing about with the modelling clay that was Polly's latest fad, Matthew slipped a newspaper cutting into George's pocket. So he hadn't forgotten: neither about the timetable of lectures nor about the promise of secrecy. Good old Matthew! George went on making an animal out of his lump of clay. They all clustered round as it took shape. Even Polly was attentive.

"What's it called?"

George quickly put his hand over the clay. He remembered his own question to Mrs Sheldrake. He hadn't been aware until then that he was making a model of the Manticora. He hastily added spikes all over, instead of just up the tail, and turned its ghastly grinning mouth into a snout.

"A hedgehog," they all cried.

"Lifelike," Matthew pronounced. "We must keep it, Polly."

After that, George took the kids down into the basement for a game of skittles.

He had to wait until he was on his own in the metal-work studio at school on the following Monday evening to take a proper look at the paper Matthew had stuffed into his pocket. That was the only place he was ever alone. He was surprised to feel that his hands trembled as he opened the cutting. It was the expected list of Mrs Sheldrake's public lectures for the season. George wasn't very hopeful about discovering what he wanted to know about the Manticora, but he'd go to one on the off-chance. It would please Matthew, anyway. George half-hoped that his idea had lost its first influence over him, but the trembling of his hands proved to him that he was mistaken. The idea had only died down in his mind, like the flickering butt of a candle, and the first breath of wind would either snuff it out or blow it up like a flame. He'd see which of these alternatives would happen at the lecture. He'd put himself in the hands of Fate.

George didn't like these thoughts. They were nothing like what usually went on in his head. Perhaps he was feverish. It was as if someone else had taken charge of his mind. Soon put a stop to that. He spread out the list on his bench and studied it. Most of the lectures were in the lunch hour or early afternoon. He'd have to choose one after school hours. They were all miles away as well. He looked again, more carefully, thinking only of practical details. The only possible one was at the London Museum on the afternoon of the day the coaches came to take the fourth and fifth forms out to the Sports Ground. He'd have to pretend he'd sprained his ankle or something. No one at school would ever believe George Fowler was missing football unless he was nearly dead. He would give up his best afternoon, just this once. It made him feel very pious, like a missionary almost, and stopped him feeling treacherous towards Matthew.

George had been to the London Museum before. It was inside Kensington Gardens, not far from the Round Pond. They had a model of the Fire of London there and he'd taken the kids to see it one wet day last summer. As far as he could remember, it wasn't the sort of place that would suit Mrs Sheldrake. Unless they used that upstairs room with the showcases of people in old-fashioned clothes. That would be all right. That would be quite a good background for a lecture on – what was it? George looked at the cutting again. On mythical miniature bronzes. What a way to spend football afternoon!

Kensington Gardens was a bit far from school and home – might be a rush, but a good thing too. No chance of anyone seeing him, of meeting anyone he knew. What could he say was wrong with him, something they couldn't prove? Sudden cramps were what that rotter Chepstow always said he had to get out of football and swimming. If they told him he could come and watch, if he wasn't fit to play, he'd plead the opportunity to work on his entry for the metal-work competition. George had always won the prize for his form, so his new form master would be agreeable. Everything at school had to be referred to form masters – everything out of school too, if you liked. They were more like second fathers, they hoped.

This year George was making a bracket for a wall lamp with a design of supporting salamanders. They were out of a picture he'd seen in one of Polly's library books. There were these salamanders which were fire nymphs, and some others called dryads that lived in trees, and nixies that lived in water. Polly had thought Matthew was interested in art when she first met him, and that she'd better swot it up. She soon discovered her mistake. Matthew still teased her about that. There wouldn't be anyone else around on sports afternoon. Chaps like Chepstow always went home or disappeared somewhere. He'd work for half an hour on the bracket, slip out to the lecture, and then come back and do a bit more work, in case any of the football masters looked in when the coaches returned. No one at home or at school would be any the wiser and George was certain he could trust Matthew. It was himself he wasn't sure of.

Every time he thought of the Manticora and his idea, he wished he had someone else to help him, or even someone else to confide in, although he knew inside that this was the very last thing that must happen. In any case, Tom and Sid were much too like Dad to be roped in. They were a couple of ordinary thick-headed boys, thank goodness. One like himself in a family was enough, George thought ruefully. Phil and Henry were too young. Polly would murder him if she thought he was conspiring to make the family feud last for ever. He had plenty of friends at school, but no special companion. He didn't need one, not with his large family. What he needed was to get away from people now and then. That left Mum. But the time to tell Mum would be when the plan had succeeded, not before. Plan! George groaned. His head was full of the Manticora but there was no sign of a real plan. He half-wished, even now, that something would happen to stop him going to the lecture. If nothing came of that, he made a vow to dismiss the idea from his mind completely. In the meantime he must keep his wits about him.

He complained of cramp in both calf muscles the day before the lecture. At home, of course, they took no notice whatever, except that Phil and Henry imitated the way he was pretending to limp, so that the three of them went along the street to school hobbling in time with each other like a trio of lunatics. There wasn't anything George could do about it, without spoiling his alibi. He was glad when he parked them on the other side of the main road – which was as far as he took them – and saw them tear off towards their gate. The form master at once sent George up to the nurse. He hadn't bargained for that. She moved his legs round in circles and he thought he had better say "ouch" and "phew" several times. The nurse looked puzzled. If he'd strained a ligament, she said, his leg would only hurt when she moved it in one direction, not all the time. She gave him some strong-smelling stuff in a tube to rub on his muscles and said it should be used after a hot bath. In fact, he ought to take a lot of hot baths at home.

George had to laugh. Hot baths! The Saturday night luxury. The two youngest had a wash down in the sink. Tom and Sid shared the tin bath, and George used their water topped up with several kettles of boiling water. Mum and Dad each had a shallow bath when the family had gone to bed and the copper had hotted up again. Polly used to go to a friend's house on the new estate as often as she could. George thought nurses and those sort of people ought to know how the other half lived, but then there was that silly young doctor standing by for old Greaves who told Mum to take a month's holiday after Henry was born. Did they think everyone lived like the Sheldrakes?

George's determination to move his family somewhere decent was renewed and strengthened, even if it meant using the Manticora. He couldn't think of any other way, except winning the Pools, but Dad was against any form of gambling. It just wasn't in his nature. Dad would wait until the end of the world for the council to move them. He couldn't understand that taking risks was fun. Not like Mum. But taking risks against the law was another matter. Persuading Mum to be an accomplice was going to be tricky.

Six

On the next day, the day of the lecture, George could hardly stand upright. Everyone felt sorry and no one suspected a thing. George was amazed, but he didn't like to discover how easy it was to deceive people when they already trusted you. Nobody ever believed Chepstow, but they all took it for granted that Fowler must really be in agony to miss football. When he made his suggestion about spending the afternoon on the metal-work competition entry, they all thought he was a hero. That made George feel doubly uncomfortable. He wished he could keep his very first idea about the *one* picture and all that luxury separate from this scheming and lying. Damn the Manticora!

He went out of the form room to the studio, remembering to clutch the back of his legs in uncontrollable pain once or twice. He heard the coaches go – the new buildings containing the art rooms and workshops and science labs were just inside the main gate. He heard the boys begin to sing as the coaches drove off. Made him feel quite sad to be left behind, to be on his own. All his feelings were twisted these days. He took out his bracket, but he couldn't work on it. Was it utterly hopeless or was it going to be his best effort yet? He couldn't decide. Waiting to see what would happen at the lecture made him feel as if he was in a no-man's land.

Mrs Fowler had asked him if he had something on

his mind, but he'd brushed her off. She was too used to the moods of boys to fuss. Even George has his black moments, he could see her thinking. Let him alone and he'll come round. The way he was feeling lately, George doubted if he'd ever come round again. Black hours he was having, not black moments. He looked at the time. The sooner this lecture was over the better. Then he'd know once and for all whether he was in for an attack of Manticora madness or whether he could forget his wicked moment of weakness, like Mrs Fowler's envious tear.

He limped out of the studio, in case anyone was watching him from the main building – that stupid nurse from the top floor perhaps. Once out of sight, he sprinted to the nearest bus stop. He didn't want to arrive too late for the lecture and cause a commotion getting in – or not be let in at all. That would be futile, after all this effort. He need not have worried. He was ten minutes too early. There was hardly anyone else there. It was in the upstairs room that he had remembered, but a platform had been put at one end and the showcases were all pushed against the wall. There was a painted screen on the platform, with a blue shawl draped across, a carved table with some flowers in a lopsided blue glass pot, a blue glass jug full of water, and a blue glass tumbler. George wondered if Mrs Sheldrake would come on to the platform dressed to match.

There were six old – or perhaps middle-aged – ladies in feather hats and fur coats sitting in the front row. He supposed they must be Mrs Sheldrake's friends come to cheer her on. George had tried to think of a way of persuading his mother to let him wear a clean shirt that morning, but she thought he'd gone batty asking for one *before* football. He'd smarmed his hair down with water and put on his best tie, which he'd sneaked out of the drawer while Mrs Fowler was busy, and rubbed up his shoes on the back of his trousers. Even so, the man on the door looked at him very warily and pointed to the back row. George took the hint. He could see the man had decided to keep an eye on him. He'd easily recognize me in an identity parade, George thought nervously, as if he had already stolen the Manticora and was a suspect undergoing investigation.

The doorman's attention, however, was distracted by the arrival of two ragged, unshaven, but very quiet and well-behaved men. You could tell they were tramps, but the doorman couldn't throw them out because they knew all about the lecture and were extremely polite. In the end, he motioned them to the back row with George. They sat down at the other end of the row, in the far corner next to a radiator. One of them went to sleep immediately, and the other one began to eat a sandwich out of a paper bag. George rather wished Mrs Fowler could have been with him. She'd have wanted to laugh as much as he did at the queer audience for Mrs Sheldrake – the ladies in front and George and the tramps at the back.

But presently a class of schoolgirls arrived and filled up several rows. Some of them pointed at George and nudged each other and giggled. He ignored them. Soon after, some earnest-looking men crept in, one at a time. They looked as if they were spending their afternoon off improving their minds. They spread out in the room as far away from each other as possible. Just before it was time for the lecture to start, a girl of about Polly's age sat down in the row in front of George, but one seat along. She looked as if she was the only real student in the place. She had masses of books which she dumped on the chair in front of him. She was holding a notepad with three pens clipped on to it in a rubber band, and had a folder on her knees with lots of illustrations and photographs and cuttings from journals. There was a label on the folder. George squinted at it, while they were all clapping Mrs Sheldrake's appearance on the platform. It said Fine Arts Diploma Syllabus.

The girl plonked the folder down on the chair and then balanced another book on the pile, a little sideways, ready to refer to during the lecture. She flipped it open as Mrs Sheldrake began to talk. There were several pictures on each page, with some writing at the side of each one. Mrs Sheldrake embarked on one of her monologues. She knew everything there was to know on this subject. George always found it difficult to concentrate in school when the masters went on talking, churning out fact after fact, not even stopping to write on the board, let alone for anyone to ask a question. He watched the student, instead of listening.

She was completely clued up, turning over the pages of her illustrated book on the top of the pile on the seat in front of him, and ticking off and underlining some of the printed part, as Mrs Sheldrake droned on. George could see clearly through the open-backed canvas chair. The rest of the audience was gazing as if hypnotized at the platform, except for the two tramps, both of whom were now happily asleep up against the radiator. George admitted to himself that it was best to be like either the tramps or the student. The lecture might not be a waste of time if he'd taken the trouble to do some homework, or needed a nice warm place to have a kip.

The student was scribbling a word next to a picture of a pair of wild goats holding up some kind of urn. He liked the look of it – same sort of idea he'd had with his salamanders and the bracket. He found he was concentrating again and suddenly realized why. Mrs Sheldrake had stopped talking. She was holding up a small bronze object. It looked like a lion to George, but Mrs Sheldrake was telling them that it was some symbolic beast with a long history and an even longer name. It dated from thousands of years B.C. The original was in a museum in Berlin and the one she was holding up was a copy only. But a very special copy. There were only four, made in a later age, but still thousands of years B.C., when there was a revival of worship of this symbolic and pagan beast. George was becoming intrigued in spite of himself. He listened attentively now.

"I realize you can't see it very well from down there," Mrs Sheldrake said. "It's too valuable to pass round, I'm afraid, even though it is only a copy. The insurance people would kill me."

There was some polite laughter, especially from the ladies in the front row. She held it high over her head. George couldn't see it distinctly, but the student had a similar picture in her book. It wasn't a lion. It was a mixture, like the Manticora, but entirely animal and not in the least alarming. It had a lion's head, a goat's body, and a serpent's tail. George thought he could knock up something like it himself, and he wondered what Mrs Sheldrake would say to a fifth copy made in the present age.

"You're welcome to come up to the table and have a close look afterwards," Mrs Sheldrake announced. "I hope you will, because the most striking feature of these miniatures is the great detail and intense feeling that are brought out on such a small scale."

George could agree with that statement. He remembered his first sight of the Manticora. He would never have thought of it as small, if he hadn't already had his idea about slipping something into his pocket. Although it had a man's head, you knew at once it would have to have the body of a wild beast. Savagery and brutality was written all over the face, although, now George came to remember it in the light of Mrs Sheldrake's present comment, the Manticora's head was no bigger than a golf ball. She put the bronze animal back on the table and went on talking about mythical monsters in general. The lecture must be nearly over, because the student looked at her watch. George had known all along that Mrs Sheldrake would never mention the Manticora. He felt partly sorry and partly as if a cloud had vanished from the sky.

He leaned forward idly to look at the pictures in the student's book again, but she was leafing through it rapidly, whipping over page after page. It was a big, thick book. She stopped at last to make a note, and there, at the bottom of the open page, was a drawing of the Manticora. It was unmistakable. Even the drawing was horrific. George clutched her arm.

"Don't turn over yet," he said loudly.

"Sssh," the girl replied indignantly. She looked round at him and then placed the book face downwards, with an affronted flounce. He was used to that kind of treatment from Polly. He didn't care. It was the sign he had been waiting for. He was trapped now. He'd made his vow and he would stick to his idea. He could hardly wait for the lecture to end.

Seven

Most of the audience formed a queue at the platform to look at the bronze animal, but the student was having trouble packing all her books into a string bag.

"Do you think I could look at that drawing again?" George asked, as she dropped her notebook on the floor.

She straightened up, pushed her long hair behind her ears, and glared at him out of her round, gold-rimmed glasses.

"Sorry I yelled out like that," he hastily added. "I'll hold your bag open for you if you like."

She handed him the book without saying anything.

"I'm particularly interested in that particular thing," George explained, opening the book at what he thought might be the same place.

"You're not the only one," the student said. "Page five hundred and forty-nine. Can't think why Mrs Sheldrake hasn't mentioned it this afternoon. The most monstrous mythical monster of them all."

"I didn't expect she would," George said absent-mindedly, finding the right page, and looking from the drawing to the girl. She was raising her eyebrows and had a sceptical grin on her face.

"I mean it's not the same as the others, is it?" George floundered on. "I mean the rest are all animal. It's the only one with a human face."

"Observant aren't you," the girl said condescendingly, sounding exactly like Polly in one of her bossy moods.

They looked at the drawing together.

"The fabulous Manticora," the girl whispered, in tones of covetous awe. She was a changed person, not a bit like Polly now. Did it make everyone feel the same then, George wondered, half-longing and half-terrified?

"Not a bad drawing," he said, and then cursed himself. He would have to think before he spoke in future. He'd be found out before he'd done anything at this rate, giving himself away all the time.

"How do you know?" the girl asked, but more scathingly than suspiciously.

"I once saw a very old photograph in a book in our doctor's waiting-room."

"You mean a magazine," she scoffed. "My doctor only has *Punch*. You're lucky."

"You ever seen a real one?"

"One!" The girl laughed at him. "There is only one. Privately owned they say. I believe it was shown in an exhibition years ago. In Paris. Or was it Athens? Lent anonymously. There's a story that goes the rounds about that exhibition. The attendants all refused to stay in the room where the Manticora was displayed. Got on their nerves, they said. Didn't like to be alone with it."

George nearly said "I'm not surprised, it gets on mine", but stopped himself just in time. Instead, he asked offhandedly:

"I suppose it's worth millions then?"

"Priceless," she replied.

64

"I didn't exactly mean that," George persisted. "I know you couldn't reckon up its artistic value in money. I just wondered how much you could sell it for. I mean, for instance, if either of us found it by accident. I mean, that's just an idea."

"You do have a wonderful dream life," the girl said, much more friendly. "We'd get anything we asked for it, that is if we found a shady dealer to take it to. Nobody reputable would touch it, of course. They'd send it back where it belonged."

"But if nobody knows where it belongs," George said, "they couldn't hand it back."

"The owner knows all right. He'd be on to us, not to mention the whole of Scotland Yard," the girl replied. "You be careful, my lad. I can see what's going on in your mind. Unless you're rich or clever enough to be a proper collector, you'll always be tempted by marvels like the Manticora. You'll long to possess them by fair means or foul and the smaller they are the easier you'll think it is. That's a temptation you'll have to learn to resist, if you're going to be an art historian."

That seemed another good alibi to George. He could always produce that as an excuse if anyone caught him being unusually interested in mythical monsters.

"I might," he said. "I haven't thought what I'm going to do when I leave school. Is that what you're going to be?"

"What else?" the girl said, as if it was the only career worth having. She put some more of her books away and then asked, as George stood silently watching her,

"Aren't you going to look at the chimerical bronze?"

65

"At the what?"

"Chimerical. Never heard of a chimera? Lion, goat and serpent. Mythical monster."

Another lecture. George sighed. He had a brief vision of himself rushing along the field, scoring the only goal of the afternoon.

"No," he mumbled despondently. "No. I don't want to look at it."

"You ought to if you're a beginner." The girl was bullying him again. "I've seen it dozens of times. Lent by kind permission of Mrs Antonia Sheldrake it says in all the catalogues."

George was puzzled by this. Why should the Sheldrakes be so proud of having their names in all the exhibition catalogues as private owners of masterpieces and then put "Lent anonymously" for the Manticora, the rarest of them all? George had a feeling there was a mystery here – a mystery to Mrs Sheldrake as well.

"I suppose," he said to the student, being careful not to ask a direct question, "if we'd collected all those works of art we'd want to show them off."

"Not always," the girl replied. "Too many thieves about these days. Experts. That's why the best things are often lent anonymously."

So that was it. No mystery. George was disappointed in a curious way, but he had no chance to ask himself why because the student was still nattering at him. Just like Polly. First she was scornful and stand-offish and then, when you took a mild interest, she talked down to you as if you were a half-wit.

"Decent of Mrs Sheldrake to bring examples of the real thing with her. Not a bad lecturer either. Knows

66

her stuff. Don't like her platform manner though. Too smooth. Wonder if it's stage fright or if she's like that all the time."

"She's like it all the time," George blurted out. He certainly was behaving like a half-wit. This was a fine beginning to cover his tracks.

"D'you know her?" The girl was astonished.

"I met her once," George said, trying to sound indifferent. "She's a sort of distant family connection."

"That ought to be useful for your future career," the girl replied sardonically. She obviously didn't believe a word.

George hardly heard her mockery. Another comforting thought had struck him. Surely Mrs Sheldrake wouldn't send Scotland Yard after even the most distant relation, let alone after Polly's brother. But then Mr Sheldrake didn't care about the Fowlers: it would hardly be a question of family pride.

"Finished with my book?" the girl demanded. From the way she spoke, George could tell she had finished with him. He handed back the book. She stuffed it into her string bag where it bulged out of the top. She pushed her way through the row of chairs to the door. George sat there, thinking deeply, until almost everyone had looked at the bronze and left the lecture room.

"Hi!" the doorman shouted at him. "This way out."

George went slowly out of the door and down the stairs, almost automatically remembering to limp while the doorman was watching. Perhaps keeping up an alibi would become second nature. He didn't much like the prospect of being a dishonest person all the time. He only wanted to do this one wicked thing that would lead to a good thing, and then he'd go back to being the same old George Fowler again – a bit of a rebel but not a sneak like Chepstow. That was what frightened him about the Manticora – he dreaded that it would have an influence over him for life. He came to a halt in the hall below, reminding himself why it was worth being afraid, thinking of the fifteen thousand pounds, of his conversation with Mrs Fowler on their way home, of her ecstatic description of her dream house, and of what the student had just told him about the Manticora.

When someone clapped him on the shoulder, he jumped about a foot into the air. Was he being arrested already? Then he remembered where he was. He looked round. It was Mrs Sheldrake.

"George! What a surprise. I always say to Mr Sheldrake that the most unlikely people come to my lectures, but I never expected you to turn up. How sweet of you!"

George's brain began to work properly for the first time that afternoon. The scent of danger had a stimulating effect. It wasn't a game of let's pretend any more. It was a campaign. He nearly called it a crusade. From now on he would be in complete command.

"Hurt my leg," he explained. "I was let off football. Thought I'd come to look at the old implements they have here – prehistoric tools."

"Oh yes. Your hobby."

"Saw your name on a poster on the stairs and thought I'd sit at the back and see what it was like."

"Near the door so that you could escape if you were bored to tears?"

"I stayed to the end."

"I'm honoured."

George couldn't tell if Mrs Sheldrake was laughing at him or not.

"I meant to have a look at that thing you held up, but I was too shy to come up to the platform."

"How absurd. You must come home with me now. Why not? Have tea. You can gaze upon the chimerical bronze as long as you please there."

George felt so queer he thought his knees would actually give way beneath him, without any acting on his part. But he kept calm and thought precisely. Her invitation might seem like Fate playing into his hands, but it was a false opportunity. He wasn't ready. It was up to him now, not Fate.

"Wish I could," he replied. "But I have to see Phil and Henry safely across the main road near their school. Then I'm going back to finish a bracket I'm making."

"I should like to see some of your work," Mrs Sheldrake surprisingly said. "I do think it's such a good idea that children are encouraged to make things nowadays, even if it means our rates go up every time they build a new school with modern equipment. Matthew showed no sign of creative ability at all, though of course he had every incentive." She sighed, but George kept quiet. It would be useless to be sorry for her, just as he had made up his mind that the Sheldrakes were robber barons and he was Robin Hood, stealing from the rich to feed the poor. "I often wonder", she continued, "what the inside of their house is like. He has absolutely no taste. It's beyond us how we've given birth to such a Philistine."

"Haven't you ever been?" George asked astounded. "Haven't Polly and Matthew ever asked you to their house?"

"Of course. I'm afraid Mr Sheldrake issues a veto."

"I see," George exclaimed. "Like Dad. There was a bust-up after Mum and me came to tea."

Mrs Sheldrake hesitated for a second and then smiled benevolently at him.

"I thought you'd understand. Perhaps if we set an example – what do you say? If you were really interested this afternoon, why don't you come to tea next week and I'll show you some ordinary mythical creatures. Not monsters. Perhaps if we could make a real contact … "

A week would give him time to work out a plan of action. At least he could take a school bag with him. It had only occurred to George at that very moment that the Manticora would make a bulge in his pocket. That was the sort of detail he mustn't overlook.

"All right," he said, pretending slight reluctance. "Not today week though. I'll be at football next Wednesday. Should think I'll be all right by then. My legs feel pretty well back to normal already, after the day's rest."

"Tomorrow week then? At four? And we won't say anything to anyone, will we? We don't want to ask Mr Sheldrake and Mr Fowler to sign the armistice before we've won the war, do we?"

Eight

That night George dreamed of the Manticora again. It had swollen to the size of a real lion and was chasing him through a dark forest. He kept losing the path and floundering among thick bushes, and could hear the Manticora crashing about in the undergrowth behind him. He was glad when morning came. At breakfast, Tom and Sid kept pushing and kicking him.

"What's up with you two?" Mr Fowler said, in his flat voice, as he picked up his sandwich tin and went out to work.

"Just like your father," Mrs Fowler commented. "Thinks he can quell a riot with one quiet word. Leave George alone, both of you."

"He knocked us about all the night long," Tom complained. "He kept on shoving, and punching us, and yelling out, waking us up. Sid nearly fell out of bed once. We tried shaking him, but he was fast asleep as that dormouse they keep pinching in that story you read to Phil and Henry."

Mrs Fowler looked at George.

"It was my legs," he said. "I expect they were hurting in my sleep. I didn't know I was doing all that. Perhaps I was dreaming. I don't remember. I don't think I'll go to school this morning. Tom can take a letter to my form master."

"I've no time to write letters," Mrs Fowler said.

"He can find your classroom and tell him. I shall have to take Phil and Henry across the main road as it is."

She sounded more worried than cross. She made Tom and Sid hurry up with their breakfast and sent them off early to give time for Tom to track George's form master down in the senior school. She tied a scarf round her head, put her coat on over her apron, and went with Phil and Henry in her slippers. If Dad could have seen her, he'd have been furious.

"Shan't be long," she said, with an uncertain, backward glance at George, sitting on the chair with the broken back between the stove and the sink. He was still there when she rushed in again, out of breath from hurrying up the stairs. He was still staring at the same threadbare patch in the lino.

There had once been blue flowers inside a red square and you could see the original pattern under the stove and up against the wall. Where they all charged up and down in the narrow space in the middle of the kitchen, the lino had turned to a brown greasy strip. Under the table pushed up against the other wall, there were some threadbare blue patches left. It was at one of these patches George was staring, making shapes from it. He thought it looked like a mythical monster. He'd got them on the brain. Mrs Fowler cleared the table and started to wash up the breakfast things, without saying a word. Suddenly she flung down the mop in the sink, so that the washing-up water splashed all over them both, and said,

"Come on, George. Don't bottle it up. Strictly between you and me, why are you putting on this cripple act?"

"You promised not to ask any questions. Not until I handed over the fifteen thousand pounds anyway."

"So that's it. You've still got that bee in your bonnet. No wonder I've been thinking you ought to see a psychiatrist. There's that child guidance clinic they threatened to send you to once, when you took against your form master."

"That was years ago. And he was enough to drive anyone to violence. There's nothing the matter with me. If I'm mental, then so are you. What about that dream house of yours?"

"I'm not obsessed by it," Mrs Fowler said calmly.

"Not much," George retorted.

"If you must know," Mrs Fowler argued, "my dream house is real, so it's no use calling us quits. The only time I'm dreaming is when I think the house could ever belong to me. But you've convinced yourself we could really buy it. Fifteen thousand pounds indeed! People go nuts like that, George, hankering after the impossible, day *and* night."

"You just wait," George said angrily. "You'll see."

"I'll see you in a padded cell. Better resign yourself to the buildings for another ten years."

"No fear. Take me to see this house, then, if it's real."

"Now?"

"Why not? Might as well make use of a day off. I don't often have one. You've taken me to the hospital, if anyone wants to know. Hours they keep you waiting there. We'd have all day and be back before the others. Unless it's in Scotland."

"It's not too far. We can make it."

Mrs Fowler didn't need any second asking. She

73

combed her hair and took off her apron. She put on her best hat and coat and shoes, as if it were an occasion. She looked into her purse.

"Enough for the fares," she said. "A cup of tea and a biscuit in a café for lunch, though. Otherwise Dad will want to know if I've been dining at the Hilton out of the housekeeping."

They were dashing down the stone stairs in no time, but Mrs Fowler reminded George to limp across the yard. George was full of questions on the way. "Where is it? How did you find it?"

"It was the day Henry started school. A couple of months ago I suppose. Just had his first half-term hasn't he? I lose count with the lot of you. When you'd all gone after breakfast and the flat was empty, I suddenly didn't know what to do with myself. There was plenty of work on my plate as per usual, but that wasn't bothering me. It could wait. I had this strange idea that everything could wait. I'd have a day out, that's what I thought. I'd celebrate my family growing up at last. I went to see Aunt Jessie in Dulwich."

"Funny way to celebrate," George said. "She's even more the keeping-meself-to-meself sort than Dad."

"That's right. Never married. Housekeeper to some institution for years. Always thought she had a bit saved up, might do something for one of you. Then she fell ill and had to retire. She can just about eke out on her pension in those two rooms. Nice place though. Nice area. Nice day I chose too. Beginning of autumn, but warm."

"Is that where the house is? Near Aunt Jessie?"

"Yes. One of those tree-lined roads. The leaves will be turning colour now. Just you wait."

74

"You're as bad as me," George said. "You haven't given up hope."

"All right. We're both mad, then. Anyone would think so, seeing us this minute. What are we doing here, George, I ask you, in the middle of Thursday morning, the pair of us?"

"We're acting on impulse, following our instinct," George suggested, thinking to himself that this was exactly what he shouldn't be doing. He ought to be constructing an infallible plan.

"You don't look very impulsive," Mrs Fowler replied. "You keep going off into these trances."

"I was only thinking", George said quickly, "that we're not so mad as to look in on Aunt Jessie while we're there."

"I should think not. I haven't got it in for the poor old lady, like you and the kids, but I wouldn't want your father to hear about this trip."

"I've other reasons for complete secrecy," George announced grandly.

"You can keep them to yourself, whatever they are, thanks, if it's anything to do with your nightmares and pretending to be lame."

They had another spell of silence after that. It was a long ride across London and they had to change buses twice, but they sat on top and enjoyed themselves looking at the scene. It began to feel like a day out. The nearer they drew to their destination the more carefree they were. They finally alighted not far from Aunt Jessie's place, and Mrs Fowler hurried them along some quiet roads. The houses on each side were quite small and all the same – a strip of garden in front, a stone porch, one window at the side of it and two upstairs. Rows and rows of them. George was disappointed, until at last they turned a corner into a tree-lined road of large houses – tall, narrow, red brick, pointed roofs, not very well looked after, but all standing on their own.

"It's three from the end on this side," Mrs Fowler said.

They were both so excited that they began to run and when they reached the house and saw the For Sale board still fixed to the side wall Mrs Fowler let out a small scream.

The house was set back from the road with some bushes along the low wall, a big glass porch like a conservatory over the front door, and the black and white lozenge-tiled path up to it, exactly as Mrs Fowler had described. They walked round the back. The side door was open and they went into an unkempt garden. And there was the old tree where the swing would be and the shed that could be a garage or a workshop.

"How d'you know what the inside is like?" George asked, after peering in vain through some tightly-fastened very dirty windows.

Mrs Fowler blushed.

"I did a really foolish thing, George. I'm not the one who ought to be lecturing you on how to stay sane. I actually went round to the estate agents and asked to be shown over. A nice young man came with the key."

"Did you tell him your name or anything?"

"I may have done. I wasn't myself that morning. I don't remember. It was being left on my own all of a sudden, after looking after the six of you non-stop.

I'd never imagined what it would be like when Henry stopped being a baby. Went to my head."

George was busy trying to prise open a small window.

"That's at the side of the kitchen," Mrs Fowler told him. "I think there was a large pantry there. I thought of turning it into my working annexe – place for the washing-machine and all that."

"What washing-machine?"

"The one we're going to buy with this fifteen thousand."

George levered with his penknife and managed to dislodge the catch.

"Could you squeeze through here, Mum?"

"I expect so," Mrs Fowler replied, as eager as George.

They both scrambled in. They walked to and fro in the house for a long time, while Mrs Fowler showed George where she would make alterations and how she'd arrange the new plumbing. He had some suggestions of his own. And with every step they took he knew he'd steal the Manticora from the Sheldrakes next week. He'd have a scheme worked out by then. He'd think of a way of selling it. He'd …

"Don't look so fierce, George. You'll frighten me. Off in one of those trances again. Let's go out into the garden. It's stuffy in here. Shut up all this time. Doesn't smell damp though, does it?"

They walked into the garden through the french doors in the big kitchen. George opened them carefully from the inside and closed them so that they fitted back locked together.

"Missed your vocation," Mrs Fowler said. "Ought to have been a burglar."

Fortunately she was looking round the garden at that moment and not at George.

"I'm lucky with the weather again," she said. It was one of those clear sunny days that come in November, sometimes, after a frosty night and a misty morning. "We could have brought a sandwich with us if I'd thought," she continued. "You took me by surprise, though."

They sat down on the overgrown lawn and gazed up at the house.

"Brickwork needs attending to badly, and the gutters," Mrs Fowler said. "Drains too, I shouldn't wonder. Needs gallons of paint. We'll need every penny of your fifteen thousand, George."

George scrambled up and pulled Mrs Fowler to her feet.

"Come on," he said. "We're going to phone those agents and see if it's really still up for sale or if they've just left the board there. I saw a phone box at the end of the road by the bus stop. Got any change?"

He copied the name and number off the board on to a scrap of paper and stuffed it into his pocket. Mrs Fowler let him lead the way, occasionally shaking her head at herself. They found the telephone box. As there wasn't another soul about, George propped open the door so there was room for Mrs Fowler.

"I suppose you can't remember the name of the nice young man who showed you over?"

"As a matter of fact I easily can. It's Greaves. Same as doctor. He introduced himself in the office and I remember now I did say I was Mrs Fowler."

"Good," George said. He rang the agents and asked to speak to Mr Greaves. He held the receiver a little way off so that Mrs Fowler could hear the conversation.

"Mr Greaves? Good-morning. Mr Fowler here."

Mrs Fowler began to giggle and had her handkerchief ready to stuff into her mouth. George deepened and roughened his voice.

"My wife came to see you about a house a little while ago. Number 55 Hethersett Grove."

"Yes, sir. I remember quite well. She seemed to think it was too expensive."

"We've talked it over. Is it still for sale?"

"Yes, it is still on the market, Mr Fowler. Rather too big for the average family these days and it's not been maintained well recently. Very old lady lived there all by herself. I suggest, between ourselves, sir, that you knock a couple of hundred off the price the old lady's relatives are asking. I think we could do a deal on those lines. It's been empty for some time now. Several people interested but they're put off by its condition. Don't like the garden being a wilderness and the kitchen being in its Victorian state. Structure's sound though. Would you like me to show you over, Mr Fowler, if you're in the district?"

"Haven't the time today," George said airily, "but I'm definitely interested. I need a large house. I've got six children."

Here Mrs Fowler had to shut the door and go into the street for a moment. She was laughing fit to bust.

"I'll consider it under offer if you like, sir, until you can come yourself. Your wife seemed very taken with the house. Perhaps if the price were reduced a little … "

"Won't be until next week, I'm afraid," George said. "I could let you know one way or the other next week."

"Right you are, Mr Fowler. I look forward to hearing from you. As soon as you've seen it and decided, we'll go ahead."

"Or I might just ring up," George said. "After all, Mrs Fowler had a very good look at it herself. I can rely on her. It's just the finance we've got to settle."

"Quite so, sir."

"Things have changed since Mrs Fowler first looked at the house. It may turn out to be possible."

"Glad to hear it, Mr Fowler. Next week, then. I can expect to hear from you? I'll just make a note of your address if I may?"

"Can't hear you very well," George said. "Have to go now. Good day." He hastily put the receiver down.

Mrs Fowler had come into the box to listen to the last part of the conversation.

"You have got a cheek," she said. "Good thing you hung up then. Whatever are you up to?"

"You'll see," George promised his mother. "Just you wait."

On the way home, Mrs Fowler was subdued.

"I've been very rash," she said. "I wish I'd stopped to think."

"You're always wishing that," George reminded her. "There was that encyclopaedia in twenty volumes you ordered when we kept bringing home questions from school you couldn't answer, and Dad made you write and cancel it; and then there was that time … "

"I ought to be ashamed, at my age," Mrs Fowler agreed. "I ought to set you a better example. Polly's right about us, George. We ought to take care. I shouldn't encourage you." Then she laughed. "I have enjoyed myself, though. It's been fun, hasn't it? That's my idea of an outing. On the spur of the moment."

"Mine too," George echoed. "But we must stop at a chemist to buy an elastic bandage to put on my leg, before we arrive home. I'll pay you back out of my paper-round savings."

Mrs Fowler looked at him nervously but admiringly.

"Say they put it on at the hospital? That's where we've been. That's real deception, George. We've never been downright wicked before."

Nine

At four o'clock on the following Thursday afternoon,
George was standing on the doorstep of the Sheldrakes' house, knocking at the door with the silver
dolphin knocker. Everyone else in the world except
Mrs Sheldrake believed he was in the metal-work
studio. He had decided what he would do. If the
trolley was already in the room, he'd have tea first and
then ask to see the swords again. He'd move to the
cabinet, so Mrs Sheldrake would have to open it for
him before she rang for the maid to take the trolley
away. When she had done this on the previous visit,
George had noticed that she had crossed the room to
pull a white rope with a gilt tassel on the end. He
would have time to take the Manticora while she
walked across the room, with her back turned to him,
and pulled the bell-rope. When he entered the room,
as soon as he arrived, he would leave his bag propped
against the side of the cabinet, pretending he was
putting it out of the way.

If she didn't ring for the trolley to be taken away
when she had opened the cabinet, he'd ask for some
more biscuits, making sure to have eaten the lot be-
forehand. Not that he was hungry. His stomach felt
very odd and every now and then he thought he
would be sick. There was only one flaw that he could
see – supposing the trolley wasn't already in the
room? In that case, he'd ask to see the swords in the

cabinet first, to make sure it was opened. Once he was standing by it, he'd ask for tea so that she would have to ring for it. When Mrs Sheldrake opened the door and let George in herself, he went cold all over.

"It's the maid's afternoon off," she said brightly. "I thought we'd keep your visit entirely to ourselves, as we agreed."

Although they went up the stairs to the same room, as George had counted on happening, he realized now that he had taken too much for granted. She might even have taken him somewhere else in the house to look at these mythical birds. It wasn't going to be such plain sailing. There would be more than two alternatives. He was a simpleton. He didn't give the chandelier or the balustrade a second thought this time. She asked him to sit down in the same chair with the gold owl on top. He had to rest his bag on the floor against it. His plan was going wrong from the outset. The trolley with the tea was already there, but Mrs Sheldrake wouldn't be crossing the room with her back to him to ring for anyone to take it away. He must think of a way of making her go out of the room, but not until the cabinet was open, of course. He could have a coughing fit. Ask for a glass of water. That wouldn't be any good, though. She might send him to the kitchen to fetch it himself.

Mrs Sheldrake had set out some birds and animals on one of the small tables in the middle of the room. That was a chance to dump his bag in the right place. He pretended to stumble against it as he got up.

"I'll put this out of the way over here," he said inaudibly, dropping it on the floor by the cabinet.

Mrs Sheldrake was bending over the table. She

83

pointed to something as George came and stood beside her.

"There was a student at your lecture who had a picture of those, holding up an urn, one each side."

"Wild goats from Crete. Agrimi," Mrs Sheldrake told him in her lecture voice. "You have a very retentive memory, George."

"They don't think so at school," George said, grinning.

She was about to let him hold a bird with a very long neck drinking out of a small bowl fixed to the pedestal the bird was standing on, when the telephone rang.

"Bother. I must answer it."

She very carefully replaced the figure on the table.

"You can start tea if you like, George. Wheel the trolley over to your chair. Don't put anything down on the carpet or on any of the polished surfaces, will you. Put your cup back on the trolley. Keep your plate on your knees. Try not to make crumbs."

"I'll wait for you," George said. "I'd like to see the pistols and things again first. I could be looking at them. I'm not hungry."

She nodded and picked up the receiver. The telephone was on a round pale-coloured wooden table. It had curved drawers to fit the circumference and painted china knobs. It was next to one of the long windows. Mrs Sheldrake sat down at the table, facing out, with her back to the room. George nearly choked. He found he had stopped breathing for a moment. He didn't like his plan being taken out of his hands like this – as if he was being used. He wanted to be in control. Mrs Sheldrake began one of her endless streams of gush. It was obviously a long-lost friend. If only he could have contrived to have had the cabinet opened before she began.

Mrs Sheldrake asked whoever it was to hold on, and came across the room. George looked up vaguely, as if he'd been examining the goats and bird with great interest. She took the key from its slot on top of the cabinet and opened the doors. The interior lit up as before, except for the top shelf. It was as if he'd made his wish aloud.

"There you are, George," she said. "Feast your eyes again, while I deal with Evelyn. It's such ages since I've heard from her. Then we'll have tea. Sorry about this. I don't want to tell her I've got someone with me. She'll want to know who. And we don't want to spoil our pact, do we?"

As if in one of those trances that Mrs Fowler had complained about lately, George moved to the cabinet. Mrs Sheldrake went back to the telephone and sat down. She gazed out of the window, fidgeting with the velvet curtain at her side, which had gold tassels on it, like the bell-rope. George bent down and opened his bag. Then he purposely clonked a few swords about, so that Mrs Sheldrake turned round for a moment.

"You can take out the ones I showed you last time, George. I know you'll recognize them. I'm most impressed with your memory for detail."

She turned round again and was soon deep in conversation. He could move about freely now and Mrs Sheldrake wouldn't turn round if she heard a noise. She'd think he was taking something else out of the cabinet or putting it back. George was surprised at

85

his own cunning. Next he looked to see if there were any mirrors in which he might be reflected to Mrs Sheldrake sitting at the table. None. All the mirrors were in the hall and on the stairs, to reflect the chandelier. She was still chattering away.

George stood on his toes and thrust his arm into the back of the top shelf. He grasped the Manticora. He stooped swiftly and put it in his bag, wrapping it round with a large handkerchief he'd brought with him specially. He half expected it to cry out, as if it were alive. He closed his bag. Then he quickly grabbed the first thing that came to hand out of the lowest velvet-lined shelf. All the time he was straining his ears to hear if the police whistle warning was sounding in the street. Everything was as peaceful as usual outside the Sheldrakes' house. George didn't stop to consider that this was odd any more, like it not being in the catalogue and lent anonymously. He was too relieved, and at the same time too concerned. How long would he have to stay by the cabinet and by his bag?

Mrs Sheldrake was saying "mmm" and "aah". It was Evelyn's turn to do the talking. George waited until Mrs Sheldrake interrupted her, and then tiptoed with his bag to the door and left it there. He'd just pick it up as he left, casually, as if it had been there all the time. She wouldn't remember after all this talk. He crept back to the cabinet. He found he was still carrying the object he had taken out of it, after putting the Manticora in his bag. He had hold of a knife with blades that fanned out in a circle, half from one side and half from the other. All the blades had different patterns engraved on them. He'd pre-

86

tend to be examining it when Mrs Sheldrake finished. He'd ask about the patterns. Were they symbolic and that sort of thing? It was just as well he'd been to that lecture. It was proving useful.

Now that he'd taken the Manticora, George felt an extraordinary calmness. He sat down with the knife in his hand and listened to Mrs Sheldrake. His mind was a complete blank for a moment, but then he sat up as if stung.

"There's only one man to take anything doubtful to," Mrs Sheldrake was saying. "He'll tell you what anything's worth and never ask where it came from. Buy it too, without hesitation. I think he has questionable links abroad. We only call him in when we want a second opinion on something we've already acquired, of course, or for a client of Mr Sheldrake's, for insurance purposes. We turn a blind eye to the shady side of his business. As far as we're concerned, he's a valuer. His knowledge is vast. If you've come across something exceptional – shall we say picked up a bargain in a junk shop – then old Vernon's your man. Basil Vernon. Bayswater somewhere."

George would need his memory if she said the address now. He'd nothing to write on. All his stuff was in his bag by the door. He didn't want to open it again, not until he took out the Manticora and hid it away safely, while he waited for the next step in his plan to fly into his head from goodness knows where. Good thing he was what Polly called adaptable, and not rigid-minded like Dad. George was going to hide the Manticora in his locker in the metal-work studio. No one ever interfered with that. He had his own key. He'd go straight there now. He didn't want to take the Manticora into his own home. He had the daft idea that evil came spreading out of it like black clouds of smoke from the Battersea power station chimneys.

"I don't know the address offhand." Mrs Sheldrake was answering Evelyn's question. "It'll be in the directory. Tell him we sent you, Evelyn."

George could look it up in the post office. They had directories for all over England there, if you asked at the inquiries counter. They'd taken them away from the telephone kiosks near the buildings, because all the kids got in and tore them up. He listened again, but there was nothing else to hear. Mrs Sheldrake and Evelyn were arranging to have lunch with each other next week. At last Mrs Sheldrake came back to the middle of the room.

"Sorry to be so long," she said, wheeling the trolley between two chairs. "Shut the cabinet, George. You know where the key goes. Then come and have tea."

George put the knife back while Mrs Sheldrake was watching him, closed the doors, and locked the cabinet. It seemed too good to be true. All the time he was having tea and talking to Mrs Sheldrake about his bracket and all the other things he'd made for the metal-work competitions, he was repeating to himself "Basil Vernon, Bayswater". He had a feeling that it was a familiar name, but perhaps that was because he kept on saying it. Then he nearly swallowed his piece of cake the wrong way and Mrs Sheldrake had to pat him on the back. She actually asked if she could fetch him a glass of water. Almost as if fate was mocking him with his own plan that he hadn't needed. Vernon. It was his mother's name before she was married. Violet Vernon. She often made fun of it. "Whoever's called Violet now!" Somehow it seemed the most important thing that had happened that afternoon. George itched to get away and think everything out. He kept not hearing what Mrs Sheldrake was saying and giving stupid answers. He couldn't have done better if he'd tried. She was quickly bored with him, wondering why she had asked him, and was relieved when he said he must be going or he wouldn't be home at his usual time and they'd want to know why. She was too impatient to usher him out to notice when he picked up his bag at the door.

Ten

When George emerged into the street, he was astonished to find it was hardly lighting-up time. He felt
as if he'd been in that room for hours. He never
wanted to go there again. He hurried along until he
came to the crescent, expecting to hear Mrs Sheldrake
chasing him, crying "Stop thief!". He hastened without thinking in the direction of home, and then
remembered that he meant to return to school, to
lock the Manticora away from sight. He turned back
the right way. He tried not to think about what he had
done, and to concentrate on the next step in his plan,
but his mind refused to work. The telephone conversation he had overheard was repeating itself inside his
head, while the open cabinet kept appearing in front
of his eyes as if he was still there, putting his hand
on the narrow top shelf and taking the Manticora
out.

He reached school just as the caretaker was locking
up. George saw him along the street, going through
the main gates. He was behind time tonight, fortunately for George. He was sometimes about ten
minutes late, but you couldn't count on that. George
often passed the caretaker when he stayed late, but
they never spoke to each other. He was a surly old
devil, not even polite to the masters. He always
attended to the main building first. Giving him time
to cross the courtyard and then the playground,

George walked sedately through the gate and into the metal-work studio. The whole school was deserted and it was getting dark now. George opened his locker, thrust the Manticora right at the back, still wrapped in the handkerchief. He grabbed hold of a handful of sketches of his bracket, in case he met the caretaker. That's what he would have come back for so late. But the path to the main gate was empty. Even so, George heaved a deep sigh when he reached the street again.

He dawdled home. Suppose Mr Sheldrake was waiting there with the police.

"Later than usual tonight," Mrs Fowler commented. She was in the kitchen. The others were all in the living-room playing dominoes. Mr Fowler always made them do this after tea every evening like clockwork. It was his favourite game.

"The tea's cold, but there's some sausages in the pan you could hot up. How's it getting on?" she added, glancing at the sketches George was carrying. He must have held them in his hand all the way home. He passed his other hand across his forehead and pushed it through his hair. Not that anything would clear his brain from the outside. He forced himself to look at the sketches.

"Not bad," he replied. "Having trouble with matching the heads of these salamanders I told you about. They've got this floating hair that acts as the light bulb socket support each side."

He showed her the drawings.

"Wish you'd make something like that for home."

"I will," George promised. "For the new home. For 55 Hethersett Grove."

Mrs Fowler hissed in her breath and pointed warningly to the living-room.

That night George took hours to go to sleep. He knew he'd dream of the Manticora and he wanted to put it off as long as possible. Also his brain suddenly began to work as if it had had a new spring inserted and been wound up tight. Hundreds of possible ways of outwitting Vernon, all no good, were milling round inside his head all night. He felt awful the next morning. As if he was a non-stop spinning-top. Tom and Sid were squabbling as usual. They wanted some money to take to school for the weekly collection. The first and second forms saved up each term for a holiday project. Everyone took what they could afford but it was all shared equally for the outing.

"I can't spare any more this week," Mrs Fowler was telling them. "Dad says you ought to be able to amuse yourselves during the holidays. When he was a boy … "

Tom and Sid clapped their hands over their ears and stuck out their tongues. Mrs Fowler gave them a clout and they stopped.

"Go on, Mum," they wheedled. "One of those new tenpenny pieces. Only one."

"What d'you think I am – made of money? Or left a legacy by Great-Aunt Matilda?"

George sat up. His head cleared as if he'd taken a magic pill. Legacy. That would be the next step. Vernon – his mother's maiden name. That was the link he had been searching for all night while he couldn't sleep.

"Did you ever have one?" he asked.

"One what?" Mrs Fowler snapped. She was flustered this morning. She sometimes said it was all too much for her and this was one of those days. But she never meant it.

"A great-aunt," George replied. "Someone who might have left you something in her will."

"Oh yes," Mrs Fowler said drily. "Half a dozen. All thinking of no one but me on their deathbeds. Left me a small fortune each, as you can see."

She waved her arm theatrically round the tiny kitchen. Tom and Sid started laughing, but Mrs Fowler shunted them off. Phil and Henry were clamouring at George that they were ready. He stood in the doorway, gazing hard at Mrs Fowler.

"You'll know me next time," she said.

"It needn't be a great-aunt," George continued as if he hadn't heard her. "Didn't you once say something about some relation of yours who … "

"There was a cousin of my father's – Henry Vernon. That's who Henry's named after. Went to New Zealand after the First World War – or was it before? Sheep-farming I think," Mrs Fowler replied vaguely, coming across the room to the door, to give Henry's face a wipe with the teacloth she was holding.

"You're supposed to be able to wash yourself now you go to school," she said. She turned to George. "They'll be late if you don't get a move on."

George expected to find a police squad installed in the metal-work studio, his locker forced open, and the Manticora exposed to view. Everything was as usual. George's headache had completely disappeared. He had the sense not to go to the studio, although he was drawn to it. He never went there during the day, except for the class lesson. It was important to behave as normally as possible. The form master said "good morning". Lessons began. Yet every time the door opened, George hardly dared to look up from his books in case it was a detective sent to take him to prison. Once he even imagined he heard the clink of handcuffs, but that was only his guilty conscience. The day wore on peacefully and uneventfully. He even managed to have a much-needed snooze in the history double period and nobody noticed. He woke up again with the same problem on his mind.

How was he to persuade Mr Basil Vernon to agree to his legacy idea? George had no doubt that Vernon would buy the Manticora, after the telephone conversation. Mrs Sheldrake had as good as said to her friend Evelyn that he was a crooked international art dealer. There was something about them in the papers nearly every day. George decided in the end that he would see what happened at the meeting in the shop. Every plan he had made so far had been altered at the last minute, and unexpected assistance kept arriving just when he needed it most. The conversation at breakfast this morning, for instance. All he had to do was be prepared to make use of every fresh detail. The practical approach, as Matthew had said.

That reminded George. There was something else practical he'd nearly forgotten. He must telephone the house agents. At lunchtime, he managed to escape without being seen. You weren't supposed to leave school at lunchtime without permission. He telephoned from the box inside the post office, in case anyone saw him in the box in the street. He put on the same deep voice and asked for Mr Greaves. Mr Greaves was only too pleased to hear from him.

"It's to confirm that I've decided to buy the house," George began.

"That's grand, Mr Fowler. Can you come in to the office to see me? Ought to have a deposit from you to send to the owners."

"I'm a busy man," George said curtly. "They'll have to wait a few days."

"Why not put a cheque in the post in the meantime?" Mr Greaves suggested. "We have had another inquiry about the house since you telephoned me last week. I told them it was on offer, of course, but I must have something definite from you, Mr Fowler. I should hate you to lose it. Mrs Fowler would be upset, I know."

George didn't believe him, but he didn't want to argue.

"I'll put a letter in the post confirming that I shall be buying the house," he said firmly, "and I'll get in touch with you personally as soon as I can."

By the time Mr Greaves began to wonder when the letter was going to arrive or if it had got lost in the post, perhaps George would have everything fixed.

"I can't keep the owners hanging about much longer," Mr Greaves said. "If someone else is interested ... "

"It's been empty for months," George said, making his voice very gruff. "They've waited all that time to sell it. A few more days won't hurt them. There's nothing to worry about, Mr Greaves. As a matter of fact Mrs Fowler is coming into a legacy. The cash will be no problem. Just one or two items to settle."

Mr Greaves was impressed. George wished Mrs Fowler was in the box listening again. He made his way cautiously back to school, smiling to himself at his impersonation of Mr Fowler. Mum would have laughed like anything. George stopped. There was nothing to smile about. Not yet. Mum wouldn't laugh like anything at what he'd done so far. He wished he could arrange everything entirely on his own, now that he'd had this legacy brainwave. He wasn't so keen to drag Mum into his Manticora madness. He'd thought before he'd taken it that it would be a relief to be able to confide in her at last, but now he didn't want her to be involved if he could help it.

He didn't want Mum to have this watched and hunted feeling that kept coming over him. He hadn't expected it would be like this, that he would have the feelings of an ordinary thief. He'd persuaded himself that his idea had been somehow different, some idiotic Knights-of-the-Round-Table task. The idea hadn't changed, but now that he'd had the courage to put it into action he didn't feel as heroic as he had expected. He felt afraid and despairing. Every time he thought of one difficulty, another one grew out of it. It was all very well having clever conversations with the house agent, but that would be a useless joke if the Manticora stayed locked up, wrapped in the hand-kerchief. He hadn't achieved anything definite, except to steal it. By the end of the day, he hadn't worked out a single solution to any of his difficulties. He felt hemmed in on all sides, almost like an animal at bay who had lost the scent of home. He didn't want Mum to share such a feeling.

As he went to the metal-work studio when school ended, he was determined on one thing. He would see it through alone. All he must do was concentrate on practical things, like remembering to telephone the house agents. What must he do next? Take the Manticora to Vernon's shop. His confidence slowly returned. He'd stop worrying and leave his mind a blank so as to leave room for inspiration if and when it appeared out of the blue. Or came from the Manticora itself in some mysterious way. That was the main thing George didn't want to worry about.

Eleven

There was no one else in the studio. Friday night everybody was glad to be out of school for the weekend. There were Saturday morning special classes and activities for anyone who liked, but hardly anybody did like. They didn't mind going for outings to places of special interest, but the only chaps who turned up at school regularly on Saturday mornings were the ones in the orchestra. They rehearsed in the hall in the main building. George wasn't free on Saturday mornings because of his weekend paper round. Pocket-money wasn't enough to buy birdseed with, so he had to have a job. Mr Fowler wouldn't let any of them do an early morning round during the week. He didn't want to be woken up at 6 a.m., especially if he'd come in after night duty. It seemed stupid to be thinking about pocket-money at all, with the Manticora a yard away.

George sat down at the end of the bench near his locker. He spread out some of his tools in case anyone came in as he was taking out the Manticora. He arranged his bracket to look as if he was in the middle of doing something to it. Might be a good plan to switch on the buffer if anyone came in. No one would expect you to look round or start a conversation if you were using the buffer. Or any of the electrical equipment, come to that. That was why not many people stayed late for metal-work. You had to be trusted to

98

use the machines and the acids and all that. Once again George was bothered by how easy it was to betray where there was trust. Stealing the Manticora had made him think of all sorts of things that would never have entered his head normally. At the moment, however, all that mattered, he reminded himself, was the practical approach. He opened the locker.

He was going to stuff the Manticora straight into his bag and dash off to Bayswater at the double. He'd found out exactly how to get there when he went out to make the telephone call from the post office at lunchtime. It was only a quarter to four. School ended at three thirty, so as to give people time to stay and do their homework in the new study and library, if they didn't have a quiet place at home. George had never seen more than about two people there, usually sixth formers. He could be at Bayswater by half past four if he hurried. He opened his bag, stood up next to the locker, and hurriedly snatched out the Manticora, still wrapped in the handkerchief. Then he sat down again and put it on the bench.

"Coward!" he taunted himself. "Why don't you look at it?"

He made a wall round it with some wooden blocks lying on the next bench. He pulled his bracket next to him, and balanced the open bag at the ready on his lap. He unwound the handkerchief. There it was, as nasty as ever. George bent over. He took a long, close look. He was determined to consider and observe it as perfectly ordinary. Then he noticed that he had his fingers crossed, like you did when you went under a ladder so as not to have bad luck. He kept them crossed while he looked, even though he told himself not to be a fool. The jagged devouring teeth were probably made of ivory – more like tusks. The two enormous flashing eyes were familiar to George from his dreams. Green. Emeralds probably. They seemed to stare straight at him, as if they knew his every thought, word and deed. George looked away and then back again. He made a colossal effort and put out his hand to touch the Manticora. He had expected it to be smooth, but it felt like the shape of a real body, with muscles. It had been properly modelled.

George forgot his terror and began to move his fingers carefully over the shape. As he did so, a way out of his trouble occurred to him. He would make a copy. It would have to be hollow – just enough time for moulding and casting – but he could pack it with some heavy substance. Vernon would be bound to pick it up. Its weight compared to its size was one of the extraordinary things about it. He could crush up some of those glass beads from Polly's old work-box she'd left behind. It was full of buttons and bits of ribbon and empty cotton reels – Henry still played with them. She'd made herself a multi-coloured neck-lace once, from Mrs Fowler's broken remnants. That would do perfectly for the jewels. He'd already bought some gilding for the salamanders' hair in his bracket.

Perhaps he could palm off the copy. He might get away with it. And then he could somehow put the Manticora back, after his mother had definitely become the owner of her dream house. George didn't care about passing off a fraud on Vernon. He was a swindler anyway, and it would serve him right. At least, that's how George comforted himself. It would just be a continuation of his original Robin Hood idea.

Poor downtrodden George Fowler against the grasping materialistic Vernons and Sheldrakes of this world, as Mum would say. But it wasn't a joke any more.

How long would it take him to make the copy? He couldn't begin tonight. He'd have to think about it first. He'd start tomorrow morning. Tom and Sid could do his paper round together. He made a few rough sketches and notes. He almost forgot about Vernon and the legacy while he planned how he would set about the copy. He was only concerned with the challenge of the work itself. He'd need Monday night as well. Perhaps Tuesday to finish off. If it wasn't ready to take to the shop in Bayswater by Tuesday evening, then he'd have to miss Wednesday sports afternoon again. The house agents wouldn't wait much longer. That would be nearly a week since he went to tea with Mrs Sheldrake. If they were going to set off a hue and cry after him, it would surely have happened by then. After a week he'd begin to feel safe. He could tackle Vernon without feeling nervous. He'd certainly need to be as cool as possible to offer him the copy.

He'd have to think of a different way of crying off sports afternoon, though. Mum would want to know what he was up to next. She'd worm a confession out of him before he was ready. He'd invent an excuse when the time came. He seemed to be getting quite good at spontaneous brainwaves. At least, ever since he'd seen the Manticora. He'd be glad to get rid of the real one as soon as he could. Everything depended on the copy. He wanted it to be the greatest thing he would make in his whole life. He made some more sketches and notes. He reminded himself that any papers connected with the Manticora must be locked up with it. He must always have the bracket ready as a cover up. He didn't care if he did dream about the Manticora now. Would give him a chance to study it at leisure. That sounded brave but, as he slowly climbed up the dark stone stairs of the tenement, he kept expecting something or someone to jump out at him from every shadowy landing. For a change, he was glad to be at home.

After the weekend, George felt even more secure. Nothing happened. No one came to question him. He read the newspapers carefully and listened to the news, but there was no announcement of a missing work of art worth millions stolen from the home of Mrs Antonia Sheldrake, the well-known lecturer on fine arts, nothing about it being the property of her husband, the well-known wealthy connoisseur. Not a murmur. They couldn't have noticed it was gone then. As George had hoped, they might not open the cabinet again for ages, not until one of Mr Sheldrake's very special friends asked to see the Manticora, or until Mr Sheldrake himself felt like a private gloat over it. George relaxed. He was able to give all his powers of invention to the construction of the copy. It went well. He'd always enjoyed making things, but this time his hands and tools seemed a part of his brain, all working together as smoothly as a high-powered machine.

He was held up on Monday night. Some chaps from the sixth form came in to borrow a soldering iron. They wanted to mend a wire in a transistor radio. George had to do it for them in the end. They were quite complimentary about his bracket, and he had to talk to them for a bit. They said they never dared come in during a lesson, there was such a fiendish row and smell. They couldn't understand how anyone could like metal-work. When George tried to explain about the machines to them, they started making silly remarks like "Vulcan's stithy" and "Dante's Inferno". He was glad when they went. The disturbance meant that he couldn't put the finishing touches to the copy until Tuesday evening, about five minutes before the caretaker was due to lock up, as it turned out.

George had seen him go by to the main building. His routine was always the same. He locked up the hall and the school and the library, then the labs, the workshops, the art rooms and the studio where George was, and last of all the main gate. After that he went home. The school gave him a free house, but it wasn't on the premises. George knew it was too late to go to Vernon that evening. He'd lost count of time, making the final spurt to finish. It would have to be Wednesday afternoon.

George took his football togs with him as usual in the morning, and a sandwich to eat at half-time. When he reached the main road with Phil and Henry, his mind was far away, trying to think of how he would escape that afternoon. It was no use hiding until the coaches left, because that had been tried before by Chepstow and he had been missed at the grounds and been sent to the headmaster and a letter written to his parents. George was so absorbed that Phil and Henry dashed away from him impatiently and narrowly missed a lorry. It was a very fast and busy main road where the traffic hurtled along, and Mum had never let any of them go to the primary school on their own. He waited to see them safely reach the other side. They turned and waved to him, but he shook his fist at them. He'd better be careful they didn't take him by surprise again. Surprise. That was it. Surprise tactics.

When the coaches came that afternoon, George went out with the others, laughing and talking as usual. It wasn't until he was climbing into the coach that he fell backwards and was smitten with the most terrible pain he'd ever had – the same place as last time, in his calf muscles, but unbearable, especially his right leg. Some of the others helped him to his feet, and the football master was called from one of the other coaches. He looked at George and obviously didn't know what to do.

"Could I sit down a minute, sir?"

His friends lowered him carefully on to the steps of the coach, and George kept his right leg stretched out stiff. They all stood round in a circle.

"Get along inside, the rest of you," the master said angrily. "We can't wait all day for Fowler. You'd better go in and see the nurse," he told George.

"He's been up there already," one of the others said. "She's no good. Suppose he can't play in the match next week?"

"Well, clear off home then and see your doctor," the master said irritably. "And bring a note, mind, for your form master. You might be the best centre-forward we can produce at the moment, Fowler, but that doesn't mean you don't have to practise like everyone else."

"Sorry, sir," George said, as he hauled himself up by the coach rail as if he had a wooden leg.

He tottered to the railings at the side of the main gate and stayed there until the coaches had driven off. He nearly did a war dance of triumph when they had disappeared round the corner, but remembered it was the beginning of the afternoon and that the rest of the school was still in the building. He could easily persuade Mum to let him go on his own to Dr Greaves tonight. There was a surgery from five to six thirty. George sometimes took the kids. He'd tell Mum, when he came back from Vernon's shop, that he'd been ill on the way in the coach and had to spend the afternoon resting in the pavilion at the sports ground. After being away last week, he'd been told to get a medical certificate to take to his form master. Old Dr Greaves wouldn't mind. He'd known them all since they were born. He seemed to like Mum a lot. No problem there.

George hobbled through the gate and down the path to the studio. Empty as usual, but one of the benches had been prepared. Someone else coming from another form to work on his competition entry. There was an art lesson going on next door as well. He'd better hurry. He placed his copy and the real Manticora side by side, for a last comparison. They looked like twins. Never take Vernon in, though. Could but try. There was only one thing wrong. His copy seemed lifeless. No, not lifeless, but as if something was missing. What was it? He scrutinized them both carefully, but it wasn't anything in the shape or the detail. He hadn't made a single mistake. It was how they made you feel. There was nothing nasty about his monster. It was a storybook monster. But the Manticora itself crouched there on his bench

105

looking more malevolent than ever. As if it could cast spells, if you believed in that sort of rot. George picked them up and put them in his bag. He told himself not to be ridiculously superstitious. That was what Mrs Sheldrake had said on the day of the first visit. But she had said she hated the Manticora too.

Twelve

George thought Mrs Sheldrake must have made a mistake when he arrived at the antique shop. It didn't look like a flourishing concern to George. The "Basil Vernon" painted in twirly gold letters over the front was tarnished and flaking. The window was crowded with gloomy, clumsy, wooden objects – dark hooded cradles on enormous rockers, vast chests with bunches of fruit engraved on them, tall cupboards with ridges along the top like battlements, and nursery chairs for babies whose mothers and fathers must have been giants. The only attractive thing in the whole window was a wooden head of an ancient man with a beard and a crown. Could be good King Wenceslas, George thought to himself. He peered through the muddle, but it was impossible to see into the shop. There didn't seem to be anyone there. The door was open though. "Basil Vernon" was written sloping across it, in the same worn-out gold letters.

Inside was quite different. George had time to take a look round before Mr Vernon emerged from somewhere at the back of the shop. There was carpet all over the floor and some tapestries of hunting scenes on the walls. There were two superb crimson leather armchairs with gold studs and footstools to match, and some glass tables with a single small statue on each. George liked a prancing horse made of a sombre marbly-looking material, and a figure of Jesus's

mother hewn out of a chunk of milky glass. He had a
vague recollection of Mrs Sheldrake talking about
obsidian and alabaster at the lecture. He moved closer
to one of the glass tables and Mr Vernon suddenly
appeared, as if he might have been spying. George
waited at the table until Mr Vernon came right up to
him.

George's vision of a crooked international art
dealer was a sinister figure in a black cloak, wearing a
broad-brimmed black felt hat pulled over his eyes, and
having his fingers covered with diamond rings. In
fact, Mr Basil Vernon looked rather like George's
headmaster – harmless, elderly, and neat, but with a
beady look in his eye as if he might pounce. He was
dressed like the headmaster too, in a fairly old
striped suit with a waistcoat, a white shirt and a
nondescript tie, and black shoes with toecaps, very
brightly polished. George waited for him to speak
first. His voice was precise and finicky, as if he was
choosing his words most carefully – more and more
like the headmaster. George easily got round him: he
didn't see why he shouldn't manage Vernon.

"You have come about the advertisement?" Vernon
asked. "The postcard I placed in the newsagents
along the road for an office boy to help in the shop on
Saturday mornings. Sweeping and dusting and tidying
my papers and running errands. You understand? I
do not require an ambitious apprentice who seeks to
learn the secrets of the trade.'

"No," George replied, trying not to sound stunned
at another unexpected twist to events. "I've already
got a Saturday morning job, thanks. I've come with
something to sell you."

"*You* have?" Vernon eyed him up and down. "I think you have come to the wrong place. Take it to Mrs Ferdinand. She has a little junk shop around the corner."

"I've come to you specially," George said.

"Who sent you?"

Vernon's voice was altered – sharp, alert.

"No one. I heard about you. I am thinking of being an art historian when I leave school. I wouldn't suit as your office boy. I go to lectures already. I heard about you there."

"Show me what you have brought."

George opened his bag to show the copy of the Manticora inside. The real one was still wrapped in the handkerchief, hidden under some school books. Vernon tapped the ends of his fingers together and gave George a considering look. His voice changed. He sounded foreign.

"It cannot be. The lost chimera. The oldest of all. The fabulous Manticora!"

George closed his bag again and looked towards the street. Vernon quickly recovered his self-control, locked the shop door, and motioned George to follow him into the back quarters, switching off the shop light as he went.

"We are closed," he said. "I keep my own hours. Sometimes I am gone to a sale. I please myself. My own master."

George followed him through a heavy black curtain, along a passage as dark and narrow as a tunnel. Vernon stopped to unlock another door and George followed him into a small office.

"My inner sanctum," Vernon explained, locking

them in. "Here no one disturbs me except by appointment."

There was a desk, an empty table covered with a dark cloth, and a safe set into the wall with as many knobs and dials on it as a computer. There were no pictures or statues or anything, except for a framed certificate hanging over the desk. It was too faded for George to read what it said. There were two ordinary chairs to sit on, one each side of the empty table, and a revolving typist's chair at the desk which was stuffed and littered with papers. Looked as if he needed someone to sweep and tidy up.

"Now. Here," Vernon ordered him impatiently, tapping the cloth on the table. "Put it here."

George could hear Vernon's heart beating as loudly as his own in the silent room. He took out his copy and placed it in the centre of the table. Vernon directed a spotlight on to it from a switch by his chair. He looked at it for a few seconds only, through a powerful magnifying glass fixed into his eye, and then he looked at George.

"A most creditable imitation," he said. "I did not know of it. You might get some money for such a copy. A considerable sum. But not from me. I don't deal in copies made by other people. Where did you find it?"

No use arguing with him.

"I made it," George admitted.

"You, yourself?"

"Yes. At school. In the metal-work studio."

"There is a revival of decorative ironwork. At its peak in the Middle Ages, of course, but the ancient Egyptians knew about it thousands of years B.C."

George groaned and Vernon looked at him rather startled for a moment.

"A respectable trade," he continued, aggrieved. "I could find you employment. You must never be anyone's office boy."

No use trying to explain to Vernon that he never wanted to hear anyone talking about thousands of years B.C. again. He tried smiling politely at the compliment, but Vernon suddenly asked him in a harsh, third-degree voice:

"Where did you see the original?"

"That's my business."

Vernon picked up George's copy and handed it to him. George put it in his bag. Vernon stood up. He moved away to unlock the door into the shop. While he did so, George swiftly placed the real Manticora on the table, so as to face Vernon when he turned round.

"Come," Vernon said, moving back into the room. "What are you sitting there for? No need … "

He came to a full stop. He stared at the Manticora. He stepped close to the table. He sank on to his chair, still with his eyes fixed on the Manticora. He stretched out his arms as if George wasn't there watching him. He stroked the monster with one hand. Then he did an amazing thing. He picked it up with his palms cupped round it and kissed it.

"How much?" George asked brusquely.

"Is it yours to sell?"

"Yes," George replied with conviction. "It's mine."

Vernon gave a very slight shrug and then started up from his chair, still holding the Manticora, but in one hand. He fiddled with the knobs and dials on the front of the safe with his free hand. He didn't like George observing him so closely and stood in front of him, but George moved to one side. There was some clicking and whirring and then several sets of interlocking steel doors, each set going deeper and deeper into the safe, slid open. Vernon put the Manticora out of sight in the innermost recess, twiddled the knobs again, and the doors closed. As Mrs Sheldrake had said on the telephone, he wasn't going to ask any questions.

"How much?" George asked again. He had his amount fixed, but he was curious to know what the Manticora was worth to Vernon. Vernon shook his head.

"I can see that this is your first deal," he said. "You are the seller. You must state your figure. Then I will say if I agree. Or we bargain."

"I'm not bargaining," George said. "I want fifteen thousand pounds."

Vernon laughed. He mightly easily have been wearing a black cloak now.

"How do you want the money?" he asked smoothly. "In tenners? Fivers?"

George was aware that his problems, far from being over, had barely begun.

"How can I take all that money in bank notes? A schoolboy. How could I use it, pass it on?"

"Give it to your parents."

"You know that's stupid," George said angrily. "You know they'll want to find out where it came from."

Vernon kept on laughing to himself and speaking in

a quiet, monotonous voice. George began to hate him.

"A cheque, then?" Vernon suggested. "Who shall I make it out to?" He sat down at the desk and pushed some of the papers away to make a space.

"Nobody's got a bank account at home, and they'd still want to know what the cheque was in aid of. I'll have to think about this. I've been a simpleton. It didn't occur to me when … "

"Take your time," Vernon said. "Anything you ask."

Thirteen

Vernon sat at his desk with his pen poised over his cheque-book, while George wondered how to introduce the subject of the legacy. Suddenly Vernon tapped impatiently on the desk with his pen.

"You have some suggestion? You are a young fellow of exceptional ideas. I should like to hear what you have to say. As a rule, I never ask my clients questions, neither those who come to buy nor those who come to sell, but this once I am intrigued. No, don't be alarmed. I have no desire to know where or how. The Manticora is in my hands now. But I must confess that I should very much like to know why."

"It's to buy a house. For my mother. You see the people who had the Manticora had so many other valuable things besides and my mother's got nothing. Unless you count six children."

"You are also a strange fellow," Vernon said. "At first I think now I have locked up the Manticora I can twist this amateur round my little finger. Perhaps I give him a little present and then send him home. Now I begin to be interested. I relent."

"I'd go straight to the police," George answered at once. "I'd confess. I'd tell them you'd accepted what you knew I'd stolen."

"I believe you would. I see you are in the grip of an idea. That makes you dangerous. So what must I do?"

"Pretend the fifteen thousand pounds is a legacy,"

George explained. "I want you to write my mother a letter saying you're the person in charge of the will." A last minute solution again. "I want you to tell her to call here to collect the cheque." As if he was being prompted by some unseen presence. Uncanny and unpleasant.

"You do not care to involve your family. You are a good boy as well as a clever one."

"No I'm not," George replied. "I'm a thief. And so are you."

He didn't want to be flattered by Vernon, to feel as if they were getting on together as people, to be persuaded that he was taking part in an attractive business transaction and not a shady deal.

"You will want to accompany your mother, I expect," Vernon said, totally ignoring George's insults. "We can include you in the legacy in a minor way. That will necessitate your presence."

"You mustn't give away that you've seen me before," George warned him. "And I don't want her to come to the shop. I don't want her to know there's an antique within miles of here."

"A boy of such ideas would naturally have a quick-thinking mother who could put two and two together. I understand."

He crossed to the opposite wall and swished back another black curtain that stuck out into the room on a semi-circular brass rail. Behind it was a door. He opened it for a moment. Outside was a mews. He locked the door again, drew the curtain, and sat down.

"This is my office with its private entrance. In front is my shop where anyone can come. People like you. In future, however, you will use the private entrance. You are one of my special clients. Out there (he waved at the shop) I buy and sell. In here I conduct my business as valuer for executors, for other dealers, for auctioneers. Executors are people in charge of wills, so that is useful for your little scheme. I have even a different heading on my writing paper for the business and for the shop."

He pulled a crumpled, yellowing piece out of a drawer and showed it to George. At the top was printed "Basil Vernon, Valuations" and a different address from the one George had looked up in the directory before he came to Bayswater.

"Is that the mews?" George asked.

"Of course. And not only a useful address for correspondence. I do not conduct much of my business by letter. It is mostly personal contact, like you this afternoon. By recommendation. The mews is useful also for my clients who wish to avoid the shop."

"Convenient for a quick getaway," George suggested, looking at the door behind the curtain.

"You are observant. Too clever and too observant, maybe. I think you must take that job as my office boy on Saturday mornings. I think I am going to insist. As part of the bargain."

"Want to keep track of me until it's all signed, sealed and delivered?"

"I see we understand one another completely. You would make me a good apprentice, even without your talent as a copyist. If you would like to learn the trade, perhaps I change my mind about sweeping and tidying only."

"No thanks. I don't want to have anything to do

with anything illegal, not after this. Once is enough."

"Oho – this letter, then? Is that strictly above board?"

"That's different. That's to protect Mum and stop Dad asking questions."

"Dad can be difficult?"

"Not exactly. He thinks there's something fishy about nearly everything, but as long as the letter is clear as day he won't want to be bothered. He'd hate to have to see to lawyers and that sort of thing. He'll be glad it's Mum's legacy."

"So what shall we say?" Vernon mused, smoothing out the crumpled piece of paper he had shown George.

"Don't be so stingy," George said. Use a clean new sheet. And I think the letter ought to be typed."

"I could take you into partnership some day," Vernon said admiringly. "Think it over."

There was a portable typewriter somewhere in the muddle. Vernon drew it out. George looked over his shoulder.

"Dear Madam," Vernon typed and then interrupted himself. "I have to be my own secretary. Who else could I trust?" He continued to type: "re Mrs Fowler".

"You must put 'formerly Miss V. Vernon'," George said.

"Her real name?"

"Yes, before she was married."

"I see. Brilliant. A brilliant conception."

He went on typing, fairly fast and accurately, mumbling to himself. "Legacy for yourself and your oldest son George. Deceased relative. Several Vernons to share. I am trustee for the estate. Come and see me at my office on Saturday morning at 10 a.m. for further information." He pulled the sheet of paper out of the roller.

"Will that do?" he asked George. "Then I'll hand over the cheque made out to Mrs Fowler and put in brackets 'née Vernon'."

George clutched his head in both hands.

"There's something wrong still. Wait a minute."

"At your service," Vernon said, leaning back in the typist's chair. "Mind if I smoke a cigar? Calm my nerves. It must be the Manticora. Usually I am not affected by these occasions."

"If you just give her a cheque," George said, pressing his hands against his head and thinking hard, "Dad won't let her spend the legacy on this particular house. He'll never be able to see it could be marvellous. He'll think the whole building will fall down the minute we buy it."

"I think I begin to know Mr Fowler. I see it is your mother you take after. She has seen the house?"

"She's set her heart on it. We've made an offer. Confirmed it. The agents know all about us. That is, about Mum and me, but they think I'm Dad."

"You have hatched some kind of plot with your mother, but she is the innocent party? That is why we must be extra careful not to rouse her suspicions about antiques? A good thing you give me a slight inkling of what is going on. It has stirred up a solution. You promise to start work for me on Saturday week and I tell you my idea in exchange?"

"All right," George said wearily. "Tom and Sid can take over the paper round for good. You'll have to pay me more so I can say I changed for the extra

118

money. I'm saving up for a new chisel and a special scalpel."

"Saving up!" Vernon looked towards the safe and roared with laughter. "Saving up, and he lets me have the Manticora for ... "

"Shut up," George said. "Leave me alone. Just tell me your idea for the cheque that's all."

Vernon puffed at his cigar, still not in the least offended.

"Some people who have much money are very peculiar. Money does funny things to people, George."

"I can see that," George replied. "There's you and the Sh ... " He stopped just in time. He'd nearly given himself away at the eleventh hour. He still had to be careful. "I mean that's why I don't want the full price for the Manticora."

"It is fortunate for me that you have principles, that you are so fastidious," Vernon said sarcastically. He seemed almost upset at last. "You will be all the more pleased with my idea. It means you will have no direct contact with the money at all. It would never do to soil your hands with money. That is for the Basil Vernons. You are the hero who braves the Manticora, who ... "

"I don't want to talk about that any more," George said. "You've got it. It's yours. All I want is to settle how I'm getting what I want for it. What's this idea?"

"I shall pretend this relative of ours, this unknown Vernon cousin, insists that everyone who inherits his money must spend it on property. He has a thing about property, or did have when he was alive. People make very odd provisions in their wills, George. They leave all their money to a cats' home, or for a scholarship for organists, or to some stranger none of the family has ever heard of. It states in our cousin's will that all we Vernons must spend our legacies on property. So I shall make out the cheque direct to the house agents."

"I'd never have thought of that," George said. "Thanks."

"Not at all. Don't mention it. Also, it will be better for me. My bank is used to such a procedure. I often buy up whole collections through estate agents, from houses that have been left full of property when the owner has died. I act for the relatives. It saves them trouble. And there is often a small treasure to be found. So the cheque will be quite in order, quite usual."

"It might be for you and your bank. For Mum it will be the most extraordinary thing that has ever happened in the whole world. She'll wonder how on earth *you* know about the house and the agents."

"George, you're slipping. That's why you must be here – to jog her memory about the house when I tell her that you can only use the money to buy property. I hope you are a good actor as well?"

"I'll need to be," George said.

"Now have we overlooked anything?" Vernon pondered.

"What about *your* family?" George asked. "Won't your wife want to know about this mysterious cheque for fifteen thousand pounds?"

"Fortunately I have no wife. This life is for a lonely man. I take risks only for myself."

"No children either then?"

"None. Perhaps not so fortunately. This is a thriving business. I make much money. I sometimes think a great pity not to have someone to inherit it. A Vernon. What do you say, George? We are related on your mother's side." He gave a sly grin. "When you leave school in two or three years, you will work in some deadly office or factory. With me there would be excitement, danger, interest and profit. Can I tempt you, George?"

"*You* can't." George pointed to the safe. "But it's just as well that's locked up. The Manticora could tempt me."

Vernon nodded, but George tried to resist his sympathy.

"I didn't expect our interview to be like this. I don't like what you're saying. I don't like everything turning out different from my plan all the time. I don't like it here. I don't like you. I'm not staying here any longer. I'm going home."

Vernon stood up.

"I forget your age," he muttered. "You come with your mother this Saturday, and next Saturday you start work. That's agreed."

He moved towards the door into the mews, leaving the letter on his desk. George stayed where he was. That was the trouble with getting angry and upset – it made you forget important things. He'd almost allowed Vernon to show him out.

"Have you got an envelope?" he asked. "And a stamp. I'll post the letter now."

"You don't trust me, not even after I have been so helpful, so accommodating? You think that would be the last you would hear of your legacy and the cheque for the Manticora? In any case," he added, grinning, "I do not forget your threat. If you do not receive satisfaction you go to the police."

Vernon had big discoloured teeth with masses of gold fillings. When he grinned he looked more like the Manticora than the headmaster. He fished about among the papers on his desk and unearthed an envelope, then searched through his wallet to find a stamp. He signed the letter and handed it to George to put in the stamped envelope.

Fourteen

George decided at first that he would post the letter at the main post office at Charing Cross, so as to make certain it was delivered the next morning. He'd had enough suspense to last him a lifetime. He could easily get there on the underground and it wasn't much out of his way. But he soon changed his mind. He was being careless again. He put the letter in the first pillar box he passed. It would have to have a Bayswater district postmark. Dad would seize any typed letter that came and put it under a microscope, even if it was addressed to Mum.

George had to exercise as much self-control as a fakir sleeping on a bed of nails when the post arrived next morning. They didn't receive many letters – a note from Aunt Jessie when she wasn't well, asking for someone to call and see her; sometimes a bill, but not often. Mr Fowler didn't believe in running up bills. Getting into debt was worse than gambling. There were picture postcards galore when Polly and Matthew went abroad, specially chosen and with a different message for each of the kids. The arrival of an official-looking, unexpected, typed letter was an event, especially as it was for Mrs Fowler. No one ever wrote to Mum. Mr Fowler nearly opened it without looking, so George had to lean over quickly and point out that it was addressed to Mrs Fowler, as if he'd just noticed. Mr Fowler reluctantly handed it over.

"What's going on?" he asked.

"Search me," Mrs Fowler said, tearing open the letter. They all stood round open-mouthed while she read it. First she went very pale and clutched on to the table. Then she went bright scarlet and looked round at them all as if they weren't there, and then she read it again.

"I don't believe it," she cried, sinking into a chair and dropping the letter on to the table. Mr Fowler snatched it up and read it very slowly, mouthing the words to himself. George nearly exploded waiting for them to say what was in it.

"Must be some mistake," Mr Fowler said.

"I shall go and see all the same," Mrs Fowler decided. "You never know your luck. I'll go there on Saturday morning, like it says."

"Who's going to look after the kids? The letter says George is to go with you."

"I'll ask Polly."

"Go with Mum where?" George asked, seizing his chance.

"Might as well let him read it," Mr Fowler said. "You others clear off now. No point making a song and dance until we know what it's all about," he continued. "Bound to be a catch in it somewhere."

"I don't see why," George said, reading the letter.

"It's obvious," Mr Fowler replied. "I expect you'll both get there and find about a hundred people called Vernon all turning up to make their claim on the estate. When it comes to the share out, you'll be given a fifty-pence piece each."

"Don't be such a pessimist," Mrs Fowler said.

"Saturday will show," Mr Fowler answered. "My

advice is don't spread it about and don't get excited. That goes for you too, George. I never knew such a pair for not taking a firm hold on themselves. Can't think what I've done to deserve it. Here I spend all my time trying to keep us respectable and here you go ... "

"Why don't you come with us, then?" Mrs Fowler suggested. "Keep us in order."

"Ever known me poke my nose in where I'm not wanted? You and George can go and make an exhibition of yourselves if you like. It won't be the first or the last time."

However, on Friday night Mr Fowler informed them that he had changed his monthly Saturday morning off. He'd be at home while they went to see this Mr Vernon. They needn't ask Polly to keep an eye on the kids.

"He wants to be there when we get back," Mrs Fowler guessed. "He's as overwhelmed as we are underneath. He'll pretend not to be disappointed and to say 'I told you so' if it all falls through, but I bet he's wondering if there'll be enough coming to us for him to buy that second-hand car we've always promised ourselves."

That was another poser – gave George something to think about while they had this talk on the way to Bayswater. How could that be arranged? It couldn't come out of the cheque to the house agents. He seemed to have run out of brainwaves, now he'd handed over the Manticora. Perhaps Vernon would have them now. George would introduce the subject of the car into the conversation, casually, and see what happened. George wasn't looking forward to his second interview with Vernon, even though it was going to lead to Mum's dream coming true.

Mrs Fowler didn't like the look of the mews. It was an anonymous, derelict place, with padlocked doors all along it, and windows whitewashed over as if the buildings were empty or used as storerooms. There were a few cats loping about and a crowd of pigeons along a gutter at one end, but no people. When they reached Vernon's door, she was truly downcast.

"What a dump! Dad's right as usual. Must be a catch in it. Never seen such a down-and-out-looking set-up. Must be a hoax. Though I can't think who would want to play a practical joke on *me*."

"Don't worry," George reassured her. "Solicitors' offices are supposed to be like this – all shabby and hidden away."

"Not nowadays they aren't. All plate glass and chromium like everyone else. You're thinking of Victorian times, George. Dickens. We read a lot of his books when I was at school. And Mr Vernon isn't a solicitor. He's just the executor. It says in the letter … "

George knocked at the door. As if he'd been waiting behind the curtain, Vernon immediately unlocked the door and held it open. George was relieved to see that he was looking exactly like the headmaster again. They followed him in and sat down in the two chairs. He sat at the desk, and swivelled round to face them. He spoke slowly and kindly to Mrs Fowler. You'd never guess the Manticora was sitting in his safe, waiting to be smuggled out of the country. He kept stopping as they had planned, so that George could say his piece at the right moment. It was like being in a play. George was disgusted with himself to find that he was actually enjoying it, almost as if the the whole thing was a joke, like his telephone conversations with the house agent. When Mrs Fowler had agreed about the cheque and the house agents, Vernon shook hands with her. George pretended not to notice when Vernon turned to him with his hand held out. They were all standing up, when suddenly Mrs Fowler gasped and sat down again.

"But whatever will we say when Mr Fowler asks how I knew about the house already, before we ever heard of the legacy?" she asked George.

"We didn't think of that, did we?" Vernon said to him, but George wasn't caught off his guard.

"We couldn't expect you to know what Mr Fowler is like," George replied coldly, and turned to his mother. Vernon abruptly swivelled round in his chair to face his desk.

"Of course not," Mrs Fowler agreed. "What shall we do, George?" she asked again.

"Aunt Jessie," he replied promptly. "You saw this house when you went to visit her. Dad's always saying we ought to live nearer to look after her. When you saw this empty house close by, the thought struck you that it would do fine. There'd even be room for Aunt Jessie to move in, if she got really decrepit."

"I'm not sure if I shall say that," Mrs Fowler objected, and they both laughed. Vernon turned round in surprise.

"You could tell Dad you didn't think anything would ever come of it, but that the house was still empty last time you went to Dulwich and it seemed such a pity. When Mr Vernon said your legacy had to be spent on property, you made up your mind to buy it."

"Just listen to him!" Mrs Fowler said admiringly to Mr Vernon. "Anyone would think he was a born liar."

"He's a credit to you, madam."

George hadn't looked straight at Vernon until then. Now he did. Vernon winked at him. It made George want to hit him, but then he remembered that last time when he had let himself be upset he had nearly let himself be duped too.

"There's one or two other details I should like cleared up," he said.

"Steady on, George," Mrs Fowler said. "I'm sure Mr Vernon will see to everything for us."

"I daresay," George said, "but we haven't explained properly about the house. We're forgetting that it only costs twelve thousand pounds. The legacy is fifteen thousand. We need the difference to pay for the builders and the furniture. We don't want the house agents to have it all."

"Naturally not," Vernon said very solemnly. "I myself as trustee for the estate will pay all the bills you incur for furniture and to put the house in order. Furniture counts as property of course, so we shall be keeping to the terms of the will."

Mrs Fowler nodded approvingly.

"I shouldn't want to go against his dying wish," she said. "Did you ever meet him?"

"Meet who?" Vernon asked.

"She means your relative. The one who left the money," George explained. "Our relative, I mean."

"About these bills," Vernon continued severely.

"You must watch your expenses, madam. Not a penny more than three thousand."

"I should think I will," Mrs Fowler promised. "And if I don't, Mr Fowler will make sure of that."

"You'll have to give us some sort of signed document to show the builders and tradesmen," George said.

"That's a fine thing, George. Mr Vernon will think we don't trust him."

"It's the people we'll be buying things from who'll think they can't trust us," George replied. "Sending the bills to someone else to pay."

"It will be simpler if I give Mrs Fowler a cheque," Vernon said resignedly.

"Yes, it will," George said.

Mrs Fowler looked nervously from Mr Vernon to George. There was a brief silence, while Vernon wrote out the two cheques, one for the house agents, and one for Mrs Fowler.

"Don't look so worried, Mum," George said. "Once Dad knows we've paid for the house, he'll have to let you spend the rest on it. You'll have to start a bank account."

"Me? On my own?"

Mrs Fowler sounded as if she'd been told to climb Mount Everest single-handed.

"You should get yourself a solicitor as well," Vernon advised. "And remember the legal fees will cost you several hundred."

"That can come out of the twelve thousand to the house agents," George said. "Mr Greaves said we ought to knock a couple of hundred off the price. He'll arrange that for us."

Mrs Fowler was dazed.

"I don't know where he gets his ideas from," she said to Vernon.

"He is a good boy," Vernon said quite sincerely. 'You have a good son. And clever too. Congratulations."

They all stood up again and Mrs Fowler and Vernon shook hands once more. George couldn't bear to look.

"Then it's all settled," Mrs Fowler said cheerfully. "We won't take up any more of your time. I want to get back to Mr Fowler and break the good news. I hope he'll think it's good news," she added apprehensively.

"There's nothing whatever he can do about it," Vernon said reassuringly. "The terms of the bequest are quite clear. The money is for Miss Violet Vernon that was, and her eldest boy. The bulk of the money for you, Mrs Fowler, to spend on a property of your own choice, and a small percentage to George here."

He was going to pat George on the head, but George ducked away. Vernon looked at him rather sadly. He held out the cheque to Mrs Fowler. She could hardly bring herself to take it.

"Mr Fowler will faint when I show him this," she said.

"Shall I post the cheque and the covering letter to the house agents for you?" he asked.

"Oh thanks ever so. You're being so kind."

George glared at him. He wondered if the cheque made out to Mrs Fowler was all right. The banks were closed on Saturday. She couldn't do anything with it until Monday. Or they'd end up with this three thousand and nothing else.

"We'll take it ourselves," he said. "Don't bother to post anything. I told the house agent we'd be contacting him. Mum and Dad can go there. And there's one other thing."

"Oh dear," Mrs Fowler said. "I'm sure we can leave it all to Mr Vernon. His time must be valuable. I think, George …"

"I want my share in cash," George announced tersely. "What is this small percentage I'm supposed to have?"

"George!" Mrs Fowler exclaimed. "Well, I never. I'd never have thought it of you."

"It's for Dad. I'm going to buy a second-hand car with my share. Property's anything that belongs to you isn't it – like a boat, or a piano. Well I'm buying a car, and I need cash. At least Dad will need cash. Imagine him ever going to the Car Mart and taking you with him to write out a cheque. He'd die of shame."

"I suppose you're right," Mrs Fowler agreed. "And he'll need transport when we're in the house. A small van now would be nice, come in useful while we were working there getting it ready."

"How much is my share I'd like to know?" George asked Vernon truculently.

Vernon went to the wall safe.

"Shall we say two hundred pounds?" he said, laughing, but not a friendly laugh any more. He sounded sinister again. He stretched out his hand to one of the knobs.

"No, no," George cried out. "It doesn't matter."

Vernon did not turn round. He barely twisted the dial. The front pair of intersecting doors slid open immediately. You'd never have guessed there were all those other compartments going back into the depth of the wall. Vernon took out a battered tin cash box and put it down on the empty table with the dark cloth, very deliberately. He shone the spotlight on to it, while he opened it.

"I think that is all the ready cash I have here in the shop," he said.

"Shop?" Mrs Fowler asked. She gave George a worried look. He was pale and trembling. He knew Vernon wasn't making a mistake this time. He was purposely taunting him. He counted out two hundred pounds in five-pound notes, put a rubber band round the bundle, and held it out to George. He backed away.

"You take it, Mum."

Mrs Fowler put the bundle in her handbag.

"Too much excitement," she said, giving George a light tap on the arm. "Time we went home."

Fifteen

"You are in a hurry now to tell Mr Fowler that he has a nice surprise as well?" Vernon asked Mrs Fowler, opening the door. "George can wait for the covering letter for the house agents, to explain everything. It will take me a little while to type it. My secretary does not come in on Saturday mornings."

He gave George another sly grin.

"I'd rather come with you," George said to his mother. This is what comes of going over the limit, he thought to himself. It's that extra two hundred pounds for Dad. Being greedy, even though it is for someone else. And even that's not true. I was more thinking of it as a bribe, to keep Dad quiet about everything else. And now here I am, not free of the Manticora yet. What on earth does he want me to stay here on my own for? It won't take him a minute to type the letter for Mr Greaves.

"I'm not sure if it wouldn't be best," Mrs Fowler said. "You're off in one of those trances again, George. I don't like it. He'd like to be there when I tell Mr Fowler," she almost pleaded with Vernon. Then she turned to George. "But the Car Mart only opens on Saturday mornings. If I don't rush it will be too late for today and Dad will be disappointed. And I don't want all this money hanging about in my handbag. The cheque's a worry enough."

"A blessing, surely, not a worry," Vernon said,

pushing Mrs Fowler out into the mews. Before he could shut the door, she stood there.

"We never thought, did we, George, that this would happen when we had our spree in the house that day. Funny you said fifteen thousand for a lark and now that's what turns up."

"Quite a coincidence," Vernon said, shutting and locking the door quickly, and facing George.

"Before you ask me anything," George said purposefully, "I want the other cheque and the letter."

"Of course."

Vernon took out the typewriter again and bashed away at it. When George had the envelope containing the cheque for twelve thousand pounds and the letter, marked 'For the attention of Mr Greaves', explaining about the legacy and the reduced price and the two hundred over for the legal fees, he asked Vernon to put the cash box back into the safe.

"You must learn to forget the Manticora's existence," Vernon told him. "You must learn the first secret of my trade. Once a deal is satisfactorily concluded, that is the end of the matter. Never give it another thought."

"You don't suppose I want to," George said. "I'd give anything to forget it. But the longer I stay here, sitting next to this table, the less likely it will be. If the deal *is* satisfactorily concluded, what do you want me for?"

"Where is the copy?"

Until that moment, George had totally forgotten it.

"What do you want to know for?" George tried to sound aggressive, but he was quite frightened. Vernon looked at him menacingly.

"In order to obtain the price I ask from my client I must convince him that there has never been a copy made in the whole world. I have a reputation to consider. That may seem strange to you, George, but when I sell a genuine article it is genuine. When I sell a fake or a dud, I do not pretend. What happens to such things when I have sold them, I do not know. Maybe they are passed off as the real thing. But not by me. Enough of this sentiment. It is dangerous for us both if this copy is found in your possession, until I have actually parted with the Manticora and it is safely in Europe. The copy must be destroyed entirely, if you will not give it to me. You must give me your word of honour."

"I'm glad you think you can trust me," George said. "Usually I'd promise without noticing, but these days I'm never sure if I *can* be trusted. That's one of the rotten things. I'd rather destroy it than keep it, but it won't be easy. My copy's a solid job. Traces might be found."

"I think we are too scared," Vernon admitted, "but perhaps you are right. We cannot be too careful. Perhaps you should put back the copy where you took the original from."

"Impossible!" George almost shouted. "I can't. I won't. It's all over as far as I'm concerned. I'll come here on Saturday mornings and do your sweeping and dusting until you tell me the Manticora's gone, and after that I'll take your advice. Wipe it clean out of my mind."

"You sound disturbed," Vernon said calmly. "You have bad dreams?"

This was too much for George. He finally lost all self-control.

"Yes I do," he yelled. "And I hope you'll be the one to have nightmares now."

He dragged back the curtain and unlocked the door himself, before Vernon could move. Vernon rushed to the doorway.

"Not I, my young friend," he said softly. "I could give the Manticora itself a nightmare. I wouldn't be in this racket if I were afraid of evil. The only thing I fear is exposure. Discovery. So you mount guard over that copy until I tell you the Manticora has gone from here. And after that it can be destroyed and we need not care about leaving traces. You understand?"

"Only too well," George said. "You're threatening me. But I'm not afraid of you. The only thing I fear is the Manticora."

He swiftly walked away up the mews, but Vernon called after him, in an ordinary voice,

"You start work next Saturday morning, my boy. Ten o'clock. Don't be late."

It was a reminder that rang in George's ears like an alarm bell for the whole of the following week. He had looked forward to putting the adventure behind him and to applying his mind to the joy of planning for the new house. Everybody else in the family was immersed in the great change in their life. Mr Fowler had bought his second-hand van. It was licensed for a year so there was no further expense except the insurance, and they could pay that out of next year's holiday fund. They wouldn't need a holiday – they'd be too busy in the house. Dad had passed his test when he first started work for the printing firm as the delivery boy. He soon became expert again after some practice in the deserted street, early in the morning.

Matthew had helped Mr Fowler overhaul the van, and had promised to put windows in the side and benches in the back so they could use it for the family car. It broke the ice between them. A little while ago, George would have been pleased to see this happening, but now he wasn't pleased about anything. He felt lonely, out of it all, while the rest of them talked about the legacy and the house non-stop. He was bothered about working for Vernon, although he hadn't had to explain at length about his new Saturday morning job – where it was and how he had got it. There were more interesting topics of conversation for the family now. He was even more bothered about the copy.

It was still hidden in his locker, but it would soon be end of term when everyone had to clear their lockers out in the presence of the form master. This was ever since Chepstow had been caught hoarding school property ready to make off with during the holidays. Was he as mean as Chepstow? No, that was petty pilfering, something George had never even thought of doing. At least he had gone in for crime in a big way. That wasn't much comfort if nobody knew how daring he'd been. Even Vernon could only guess. Whenever George looked at the copy, he couldn't bring himself to throw it away. It was really something outstanding. He wished there was someone he could show it to, before he destroyed it, someone who could appreciate it. George was proud of his work, but he'd have to decide soon what to do about it, before the Christmas holidays. Mum wanted to move in then, although the house wouldn't be anywhere near ready and in a terrible mess. She wanted to be on the spot, to keep the workmen under her thumb, and she wanted to leave the buildings as soon as she possibly could.

She was on the go all day long, backwards and forwards to Dulwich. It was hard to remember these days that he had ever seen her shed a tear. He couldn't ruin her happiness now by going back on his vow to go it alone, although he did wish he had someone to talk to about the copy. Sometimes he wondered if he could approach Matthew in a roundabout way, but that might remind him of the lecture, which he hadn't referred to since and which George hoped he had forgotten. On the Friday at the end of the week, Polly and Matthew arrived unexpectedly. George had a vague hope that he might perhaps be able to speak to Matthew on his own somehow. He could ask his advice about pulverizing metal objects for instance – an engineer ought to know about that. There might be a way of utterly destroying the copy and leaving no trace.

One look at Matthew was enough to make George realize that he couldn't possibly tackle him then. Matthew looked terribly upset.

"We've come to let you know I shan't be able to take you to Dulwich tomorrow morning first thing, after all."

Polly and Matthew were going to have their first look at the house. They were taking Mrs Fowler and Phil and Henry in the Mini. Tom and Sid were doing George's paper round, George would be at his new job, and Mr Fowler would be at work, so they were all going in the van at midday. If George wasn't home in time, he could come on the bus in the afternoon.

Earlier in the week, Mrs Fowler had suggested that Mr Fowler took the week off and came with her to the agents to arrange everything.

"I took last Saturday morning off out of turn," he said, "and that's my lot."

He'd looked at her as if she'd asked him to fly to China and back for the day. She didn't insist. It was a weight off her mind and George's too. They had been dreading that Mr Greaves would say something about the telephone conversation when Mr Fowler was there. So that was another danger removed.

But Mrs Fowler had been looking forward to showing off her purchase to Polly and Matthew. She wanted to ask their opinion about her plans. They were both good at that sort of thing.

"I'm sorry to let you down," Matthew said, seeing her disappointed look. "And I'm sorry Polly can't take you herself, but I'll need the car. It's my father."

George began to walk out of the living-room into the kitchen, and then stopped in the doorway. No good running away from the Manticora. Everyone had stopped talking and they were all looking at Matthew. He hardly ever spoke to them about his parents, not when they were all together like this.

"He's quite ill, apparently. Mother rang me up yesterday. She wants me to go tonight. We're on our way. We may have to stay the weekend. Mother sounded frantic. He's not eating or sleeping and he's cancelled all their social engagements. She was so worried she telephoned his office and they said he'd hardly been there. She asked him about it and he confessed that he'd been walking about the streets, but he wouldn't say what was on his mind. I've no idea what she expects me to do. He's not likely to confide in me. We've never been very close, as you know. But I feel I must at least answer the S.O.S."

"Wouldn't be natural if you didn't," Mrs Fowler said. "The house can wait. I'm sorry."

So was George, but he didn't say so. He was glad when Polly and Matthew left.

Sixteen

Mrs Fowler decided to go early on the bus herself to Dulwich and to take Phil and Henry with her. They could play in the garden while she did some measuring. The contract hadn't been signed yet, but when Mr Greaves had received Vernon's cheque and letter he let Mrs Fowler have a key; the house was standing empty; Mrs Fowler had a lot to do before they could move in so she might as well begin. He was going to settle the legal side of it as quickly as possible for her. He kept saying he was looking forward to meeting Mr Fowler, but Mrs Fowler pretended she was too busy to pay much attention. She'd told George about this and they were glad for once that Dad didn't like meeting new people. She'd even taken Aunt Jessie to see the house.

"Guess what she said, George?"

George had to make an effort these days to join in Mum's light-heartedness.

"Just what you'd expect," Mrs Fowler continued, without waiting for an answer. "'Mr Fowler must be mad to let you throw your money away like that. If it was my legacy, I'd buy a nice new little bungalow near the shops.' Just you wait, I told her, you'll see."

George remembered how often he had said that to his mother when he first thought of his idea. He'd remembered and thought a lot during the night, after Matthew's arrival to tell them about his father. He

141

felt sure there was some connection between Mr Sheldrake's illness and the Manticora. He thought about it all the way to Vernon's shop. Vernon was very ordinary and businesslike. Obviously nothing had happened there. Strange.

"You're very absent-minded this morning," Vernon said. "Not been sleeping well?"

"It's nothing to do with you," George said. "I'll be here on time and I'll do everything you tell me as best I can, but I'm not going to answer a single question."

"A pity. I should like to have asked you how the house is going, and whether Mr Fowler bought his motor, and ..."

"What must I do first of all?" George rudely interrupted.

Vernon handed him a duster.

"Everything in the shop and the window must be cleaned, except those."

He pointed to the two statues George had admired when he came to sell the Manticora – the prancing horse and the madonna.

"Those I do myself. This morning I shall leave you to dust the whole shop, and next week you can begin clearing out the office."

"What shall I do if a customer comes?" George asked.

"I am only going into the office. You ring this bell. Be very polite, please, but never answer any queries yourself. Always send for me at once."

"There's someone coming now, I think," George said. "Don't go yet."

They stood together in the middle of the shop, George holding the duster and Vernon pulling down his rumpled waistcoat and smoothing back his hair. A lady opened the door. It was difficult to see her face against the bright light coming into the dim shop from the street. She advanced quickly down the middle of the shop, holding out her hand to Vernon. He smiled and put out his own hand as she drew nearer, but she didn't take it. She saw George and came to a halt, dropping her hand to her side. It was Mrs Sheldrake. George panicked and said the first thing that was in his head, that had been there all night and all that morning.

"How's Mr Sheldrake? Matthew said ... "

And then he became conscious of Vernon staring at him with a cynical, knowing twist to his lips, not quite smiling. When Mrs Sheldrake began to speak, he looked at her in the same way.

"He refused to see Polly as usual. Shut himself up in his room. They stayed the night, though, to keep me company, and they're in the house now. It's not wise to leave him on his own at the moment."

She gave a tearful smile and seemed to be trembling a bit. Matthew had said she was frantic, but she didn't seem to be all that changed to George. She was still treating him and Vernon in her grand manner, but he did sense that, underneath, she was almost appealing to them for help. Vernon's expression was now completely deadpan, as he looked from George to Mrs Sheldrake. He showed neither interest nor surprise. He was ready for anything without comment. If that was another secret of the trade, George was glad he wasn't going to be an apprentice.

"Did Polly mind?" he asked. That was what he was thinking and he wasn't going to hide it, like Vernon.

"In the past she's been more proud than hurt, but when she came last night she was really concerned. She's been most helpful. She's an excellent little cook. Later on, when they'd gone to bed, Mr Sheldrake talked to me for a long time. I think he was touched by their coming." She continued to address George, but Vernon was listening eagerly to every word, in spite of appearing to be discreet in the background. "Perhaps he was impressed by the soufflé Polly made to tempt him to eat – he was taken aback when I told him who had cooked it. Whatever it was, he lowered his defences, he talked, he told me … "

She broke off, began to speak again, and then stopped, as if she had something she would like to say to them, but daren't. Then she recovered herself and took a second look at George.

"But however did you find your way here?"

"My advertisement in the paper shop. He is my new office boy. I never expected to discover he would be known to my favourite customer, well, customer is hardly the word," Vernon swiftly replied.

"We're very slightly related," Mrs Sheldrake said curtly.

"Even better. I have chosen the right boy. With such a connection, however distant, he cannot fail to suit the antique business."

"I'm only related by marriage," George said.

"I see." Vernon's lips had the cynical smile on them again. "I see. That's how it is."

"Whatever you see and however it is," Mrs Sheldrake flashed at him, quite in her usual haughty way, "it's hardly your affair – not your business, I should have thought."

144

"Ah, business!" Vernon sighed. "You have come about business, and here I was hoping we were three friends. However … "

He shrugged, spread out his hands, and waited for Mrs Sheldrake to speak. She became extremely jumpy again. George moved away, unfolding his duster, but Vernon gently grasped him and pulled him back.

"Wait now. There may be something you must fetch to show Mrs Sheldrake. This is your first customer. You must learn what there is to do, in case I am called away, how to behave." He turned to Mrs Sheldrake. "His first morning with me. I engage him some ten days ago, but he starts only now."

He paused for a moment, almost purposely George suspected, but Mrs Sheldrake didn't connect. She gave one of her slightly embarrassed artificial laughs and said,

"In fact, I didn't come as a customer. Just a friendly visit as usual. Forgive my ill manners. I'm rather worried about Mr Sheldrake. However, my personal affairs are not your concern."

She was making a tremendous attempt to hide her tension.

"Please convey my best wishes for his speedy recovery," Vernon said politely. "And now what can I do? How can I have the pleasure of assisting you?"

Mrs Sheldrake looked round the shop in a distracted way and answered Vernon without looking at him. George could hardly hear her. He moved closer. He had no urge to escape now. He was beginning to feel sorry for Mrs Sheldrake. Vernon didn't

145

care a scrap. He almost seemed to be torturing her for the sake of it.

"Only a casual visit," Mrs Sheldrake mumbled. "Happened to be passing. Wondered if anyone had brought anything interesting to you lately. Looking for material for my lectures. Think I'm becoming stale."

She let her glance rest on George. He felt his heart thumping again as it did when he brought the Manticora to Vernon. He remembered it was there, in the safe, at the back of the shop. He could feel that Vernon had held his breath for a second. Vernon knew what had happened for certain now.

"I'd completely forgotten you came to my lecture, George. I suppose that's why you chose an antique shop for your pocket-money job."

She was obviously recalling everything about that afternoon, remembering how she'd asked him to tea the following week. He was sure she was seeing the open cabinet in front of her eyes, just as he had done. She was looking at him in a puzzled, disbelieving way.

"No swords or pistols here, George," she said, trying to be cheerful.

"I've had nothing new at all, nothing," Vernon replied rapidly, pushing George away now. "Prices are too good at the sales lately. Everything is sent to the salerooms, unless I have a lucky chance."

"I only wondered," Mrs Sheldrake said, forgetting about George. She was vague and half-apologetic. "I recommended a friend to you recently. I thought she might have brought something in. She wasn't satisfied with the valuation they'd given her at the sale-room. Evelyn Martin. Writes for *Country Life* –

those articles about old furniture in castles open to the public."

Vernon shook his head.

"A stranger to me."

"I'm surprised she hasn't been. She telephoned me not long ago especially to ask me where to go with …"

Mrs Sheldrake stopped and gasped. She looked at George, no longer puzzled but disturbed, and then at Vernon.

"No," she whispered to herself. "It's not possible. It can't be." She took a deep breath and tried to speak in her everyday voice. She looked straight at George, accusingly. "That was the day you came to tea. I remember absolutely every detail of that afternoon. It's been in my subconscious, waiting to be dragged to the light. You were standing by the cabinet. Your school bag was on the floor next to you. Then I had a long conversation with Evelyn, with my back to you. I was telling her about Basil Vernon. Somewhere in Bayswater I said. You were listening. You had already taken the Manticora. But why … how … ?"

George thought the floor of the shop was moving beneath him and that the tapestries on the wall were swaying to and fro. Then he thought he might faint. He wondered why he didn't fall. He felt weak and dizzy. Then he realized that Vernon was holding him firmly by the elbow, almost propping him up. Before either of them could say anything, Mrs Sheldrake suddenly broke down.

"It's you," she screamed at Vernon, pointing at him. "You planned it all. You made George steal the Manticora. It's here. You've got it. I know you have.

You must give it back. I'll pay you anything. Anything. I must have it back."

She was openly crying now and beating on the nearest piece of furniture and stamping her feet. When Polly went off her head like that once or twice at home, before she was married, Mrs Fowler had always given her a hard slap to bring her round.

"Take Mrs Sheldrake into my office and let her sit down. I'll lock up the shop," Vernon said very quietly and smoothly. "We must clear up this little mis-understanding."

Seventeen

George helped Mrs Sheldrake through the curtain and along the passage into the inner sanctum. He pulled one of the chairs towards her and she sank into it, sobbing and moaning. Then she leaned her arms on the empty table with the dark cloth and rested her head on them. George didn't know what to do. He was glad Vernon was only away for a minute. As soon as he came into the office, and spoke to Mrs Sheldrake, it started her off again. She sat up, still moaning.

"What am I to do? Help me, help me. Give me back the Manticora. It's not for me. I'd be ashamed to behave like this for myself. It's my husband. It's Mr Sheldrake. Oh, why did he do such a thing? What possessed him? He'll be ruined. Utterly discredited. It couldn't be worse for his name and reputation if he'd committed murder."

"That's a bit thick," George blurted out. "I mean nothing's worse than murder."

It was a daft thing to say, but he couldn't think of anything else and Vernon was just standing there, as if she was reading out a shopping list. George's disconnected remark brought Mrs Sheldrake to her senses. She stopped ranting. She wiped her eyes and blew her nose. She sat very still for a moment. Then she said, in her usual Sheldrake voice,

"I shall have to tell you everything now. It's a long story. You might as well sit down."

Vernon sat opposite Mrs Sheldrake and motioned George to the swivel chair at the desk. George was glad not to be facing Mrs Sheldrake. Vernon was cool and unmoved. George felt awful. There was another silence, but it wasn't a true silence. The shabby, dusty little room was filled to the corners with suspense. And all the time, there was the Manticora beside them, in the safe. Finally Mrs Sheldrake spoke in an exhausted, expressionless voice.

"You see – the Manticora doesn't belong to Mr Sheldrake. He stole it himself."

"You are making a slight mistake," Vernon said, equally expressionless. "You tell us the Manticora doesn't belong to Mr Sheldrake. That is the present. Surely you must say it did not belong to him. In the past. Not the very distant past, as George can witness."

George was wishing he could sort everything and everyone into two separate piles – black and white. He had thought his idea of taking from the Sheldrakes was all right, because they were so rich and Mum was so poor, and because they had been horrid to Polly. Now he was thinking perhaps Mrs Sheldrake wasn't so nasty after all. He was hating Vernon again, but then there were times when Vernon seemed not a bad chap. George had never been troubled with thoughts like this before he stole the Manticora. He'd never had to ask himself whether what he was saying or doing was black and white or right or wrong. He used just to do things, and say things. Perhaps that was best, after all.

"I did steal the Manticora that afternoon," he said to Mrs Sheldrake, "and I did bring it here. No one put me up to it. It was my own idea. I'm not Vernon's stooge. It was because of all your things, and Polly and Matthew, and Mum crying, and the tenement, and Dad being so stiff-necked … "

Mrs Sheldrake wasn't listening. She totally ignored George. She didn't even turn aside to look at him.

"Is it sold yet?" she asked Vernon. "Let me buy it back from you. Please. I beg you."

"It is already promised. I do not go back on my word. In any case I cannot. The man who takes it is my best connection in Europe. I cannot afford to disappoint him. And think how you would put yourself in my power. I could never resist such a temptation to blackmail. I am such a villain. Ask George. Better that we say nothing together. Better that we have honour amongst thieves."

Mrs Sheldrake stood up angrily. For a moment George thought she was going to punch Vernon on the nose, but she thought better of it. Vernon politely waited until she sat down again, before he continued his speech.

"I do not know how long Mr Sheldrake has been, shall we say, the caretaker of the Manticora. Long enough, I presume, for the rightful owner to have given up hope of recovering it."

"Craigmyle," Mrs Sheldrake muttered. "Alexander Craigmyle. He was the rightful owner."

"He was the man Mr Sheldrake stole it from?" Vernon asked blandly.

"I shouldn't have said he stole it. It's not quite like that. You make him sound like a common thief."

Mrs Sheldrake was very agitated. George began to see what Matthew meant when he had called her "frantic".

"Like George here, and myself," Vernon said, and was pleased when George grinned, in spite of himself.

All the time George was divided between the two of them. First he thought he was on Mrs Sheldrake's side and then he thought he was on Vernon's side. He kept losing sight of the fact that he was the culprit, that he would be in as much trouble as Mr Sheldrake in the end. He'd better listen to what they were saying. It was going to be very important for him.

"I remember Alexander Craigmyle," Vernon said. "He had a flair for discovering minor masterpieces that everyone else had been searching for in vain. That was a queer collection he accumulated. Every piece in it had some legend attached, or had been used in idol worship. We have all heard of Craigmyle's chimerical beasts."

George let his attention wander. If it was going to be a long chat about mythical monsters, that wouldn't be much use. He wondered what Mum and Phil and Henry were doing at this very moment. Phil and Henry would be climbing the old tree in the garden, and Mum would be roaming round the house, her head full of visions of what it would be like when it was all done. No, he wasn't sorry for anyone. He was glad he'd stolen the Manticora. He listened again to the conversation, not caring what they said now, or what trouble was in store for him.

"Craigmyle made good in Canada as a young man," Mrs Sheldrake told Vernon, "but it was always his ambition to leave his unusual and valuable collection to the museum in his home town in Scotland."

"Didn't Mr Sheldrake help the curator of that museum with an exhibition of the collection, shortly after Craigmyle died? I seem to recall reading something some years ago. It all comes back to me," Vernon said dreamily, but with the pouncing beady look in his eye more marked.

"So will it all come back to the curator of that museum," Mrs Sheldrake said mournfully. "That's what frightens my husband, makes him talk in his sleep, when he gets any sleep."

Vernon half turned to look at George, with the cynical smile. He kept trying to include George, but Mrs Sheldrake seemed to have forgotten he was there.

"And so Craigmyle acquired the Manticora at last," Vernon mused, not caring about Mrs Sheldrake's worries, but anxious to hear the whole story. "I imagine he acquired it honestly, not like George and Mr Sheldrake?"

"What about you?" George said sullenly.

"I have paid well for it," Vernon replied.

"Not so much as you'll get for it, I bet," George said.

"Not quite," Vernon said, almost laughing. "But we interrupt Mrs Sheldrake. It is most interesting, about Craigmyle."

Mrs Sheldrake had lapsed into a worried coma while George and Vernon argued. She made another effort to produce her usual air of unflappability.

"Craigmyle was a much travelled man," she began again, using her lecture voice, as if it were a kind of protection against breaking down. "He was known to archaeologists all over the world. Everyone knew it was his ambition to add the Manticora to his collection. The Manticora would be the king of all those ghastly, unnatural, revolting objects. Craigmyle made a fortune – something to do with a new kind of corn-flake – and he spent that fortune on the search. But nobody knew for certain if and when he ever found the Manticora."

"Nobody but Mr Sheldrake, apparently," Vernon observed.

"Mr Sheldrake was Craigmyle's business adviser. Craigmyle was perfectly capable of managing the cornflake invention, but he had no idea what to do with the fortune he had made, except that he wanted to invest it to make more money to spend on his collection and the search for the Manticora. Mr Sheldrake advised him about shares – we have important links in Canada and America."

She came to a stop and buried her face in her hands, moaning: "Oh God, whatever will they say? Chairman of the board of directors, one of the oldest firms in the City … "

"Too bad," Vernon said, "but if we all keep quiet, as I suggest, and the Manticora leaves the country for an unknown destination, then Mr Sheldrake's firm will be none the wiser."

George was about to say something, but Mrs Sheldrake began to talk in her lecture voice again at the same time. She seemed to pull herself together every time he was rude to her. In a way, it was the same treatment as Mum slapping Polly to bring her round after a screaming and stamping fit, but George didn't think that Vernon meant well. He seemed to be taking the opportunity of getting his own back on the Sheldrakes for all the years they'd patronized him. That was something else George could understand, when he remembered the day when he went to tea with

Mum. And yet he was glad that Mrs Sheldrake was able to stand up to Vernon. If he ever got out of this mess, he'd stick to football and metal-work.

"Mr Sheldrake and Craigmyle were more than business associates. When they discovered they both had collector's mania, they became great friends. Mr Sheldrake often went to Canada to see him, apart from business. Craigmyle was a lonely man. No family. No friends. Never married."

"Like me," Vernon said to George.

"He was a hard, dour and unimaginative man," Mrs Sheldrake continued.

"Ah, not so like me," Vernon said with a smile. "I suppose that was why he was unaffected by the stories surrounding his collection. There were many articles about this. Most interesting. African masks that could kill your enemies, Indian statues that could make the crops of your neighbour wither if he let his cow loose on your land, Mexican gods that could summon a storm."

"Those were the more ordinary ones," Mrs Sheldrake said. "Some had an evil power that could send a shiver down your spine. But even the Manticora was no more to Craigmyle than the desirable crown of his collection. I always hated having it in the house myself."

"I have a theory," Vernon said. "Perhaps this Craigmyle was a good man. Perhaps only truly good people ... "

"Mum didn't seem to think anything of it," George said reflectively.

"Nonsense," Mrs Sheldrake said briskly. "Craigmyle was simply a very unemotional man. I suppose that's why he got on so well with my husband. They were very close at the end."

"So that when Craigmyle died and left his collection to the museum in his home town in Scotland, Mr Sheldrake was in a position to hand over everything except the Manticora?" Vernon guessed. "Not exactly stealing, of course. Simply taking advantage of his position of trust as Craigmyle's only friend and sole executor."

"It will be the last time he'll ever be in such a position," Mrs Sheldrake said sorrowfully. "He'll have to give up all his public appointments, of course. It will be a disaster, as I said."

"I do not see why," Vernon said again. "That curator has only a hunch surely? He has heard, like everyone else, that the Manticora was somewhere in Canada and that Craigmyle had been searching for it, but there was nothing definite known at any time."

"He has more to go on than that," Mrs Sheldrake admitted. "Craigmyle had promised him a list of everything. Mr Sheldrake said this had been lost. There was nothing the curator could do. Mr Sheldrake, as you surmised, was in sole charge of everything outside the cornflake business. In a position of trust and friendship, as you so rightly point out. Ever since Craigmyle's death, that curator has always appeared at Mr Sheldrake's elbow at auctions and exhibitions and private sales. He came to one of my lectures – the same one you heard, George. Mythical monsters. He knew that was Craigmyle's chief interest. I couldn't think why he seemed to be keeping an eye on us. He's never left us alone."

George knew that feeling. Hunted and watched.

156

He could sympathize. He had thought he was free of that, or would be when Vernon didn't want him in the shop any more on Saturday mornings and the Manticora had gone from the safe, but he feared that it might be beginning all over again.

"If Mr Sheldrake were to inform the police that the Manticora had been stolen, he would also have to inform them that it wasn't insured. That's the first thing they'd ask. Whatever excuse Mr Sheldrake gave the police for such an oversight on the part of an experienced collector who was so fussy about his burglar alarm and catalogue for everything else, that curator would know the real reason at once. He'd know that Mr Sheldrake couldn't have insured stolen property."

"There are methods," Vernon said. He turned to George. "Another secret of the trade. Let me persuade you again. You are meant for it. Not insured. The original list destroyed. Not in the Sheldrake catalogue. You are a genius."

"He's a scoundrel and so are you," Mrs Sheldrake retorted. "I must go. It was absurd to come here. What am I doing? Why am I telling you all this?" She started to weep again. She shouted at George. "And if you think Matthew is fond of you and of the rest of your family, what is he going to think now? He'll know I was right. That it was a mistake to marry a type like Polly."

"And what will Polly think of Matthew's family," George answered back, angry and ashamed. "What will she think when she hears that Mr Sheldrake ... "

"They will think the same as they have always thought, this Polly and this Matthew," Vernon interrupted. He was laughing at them. "Mr Sheldrake will not be so foolish as to inform the police. That curator will never know what has happened to the Manticora. I am the only person who will know that. Everything we are saying here is between these four walls. They are used to keeping secrets, these walls. Polly and Matthew, whoever they are, will never know what has passed here this morning. So calm yourselves."

"You won't be so calm when Mrs Sheldrake tells you what's really driving them dotty," George told Vernon. "He's probably glad to be rid of the Manticora in a funny kind of way. I know how he feels. But she isn't telling you the worst. Other people have seen the Manticora in the Sheldrakes' house. Mr Sheldrake has shown it to some friends. What are they going to think if they ask to see it and it's gone and Mr Sheldrake hasn't informed the police? He might put them off once or twice, saying it's being cleaned, or lent, or kept in the bank or something, but not for ever. They'd get suspicious. I thought there was some mystery myself, but these friends will be people who know a lot about antiques, I expect, or he'd never have wanted to risk showing it off to them. If he pretends it's lent to an exhibition, they'll want to know which one, even if he does put 'lent anonymously' for the public."

"No, that was Craigmyle," Mrs Sheldrake couldn't help correcting him, even in her distress. "That was long ago."

Vernon was grinning broadly with delight. He was rubbing his hands.

"Better and better," he said merrily. "I shall make the biggest profit of my life and there is no risk. No

158

risk at all. Now we have *all* the truth. Mr Sheldrake doesn't know which way to move. That is why he has not moved yet. Why you have been fortunate, George, as well as I. If Mr Sheldrake does inform the police of his loss, that curator will swiftly act. If Mr Sheldrake neglects to inform the police, then his privileged friends will ask awkward questions. He is in a cleft stick. Meanwhile, Mrs Fowler has her house and my client will arrive and I shall complete the sale. How very foolish but how very convenient of Mr Sheldrake to have shown the Manticora to anyone at all when it did not rightfully belong to him. But you have always been, if I may say so, rather boastful about your possessions, Mrs Sheldrake."

"Scoundrel!" Mrs Sheldrake spat at him. "Forger! I've proof of that. I'll expose you. You won't get away with this."

"The Manticora is there in my safe. Start an investigation and my shop will be searched for evidence. There will be such publicity. My pathetic attempts at patching up an odd fake or two to sell for a few pounds, quite straightforwardly, to those who cannot afford the real thing, will be lost sight of in the glare of the scandal of the Manticora. That curator, the board of directors, your friends, the societies who ask you to lecture ... "

Mrs Sheldrake blindly charged against the door into the corridor between the office and the shop.

"Let me out. Let me go," she was crying.

"Open the door. Quick," George said angrily to Vernon, who was standing quite still and silent, watching Mrs Sheldrake fling herself about the tiny office like a bird trapped indoors. "She'll hurt herself," George almost shouted, giving Vernon a heave with his shoulder in the direction of the door.

Vernon gave him a reproachful look.

"I shall look after her. You will see. No need for these rugby tackles."

"Rugby!" George replied scornfully, but Vernon was occupied in calming Mrs Sheldrake, making her sit down again. What was he up to now? Why didn't he just let her go? There was nothing more to be said or done. They were all slaves to the Manticora now.

Eighteen

"I think I'll sit down too," George said. He didn't like the cat-and-mouse way Vernon was looking at Mrs Sheldrake: and cat and mouse didn't describe his look at all. It was more like snake and rabbit. Mrs Sheldrake was looking back at Vernon as if she was wondering what was coming next too. They were both bewildered when he gave one of his rare, teeth-baring, Manticora smiles.

"It will be all right. Everything will be all right. I have a brainwave, Mrs Sheldrake. Not so much my brainwave. I only remember. The credit must go to George."

"If you've anything of value to suggest," Mrs Sheldrake said, in her ordinary voice, "I wish you'd come directly … "

"The value will be for you to decide," Vernon interrupted. He turned to George. "We are safe now, my boy. Quite safe from the arm of the law. Mr Sheldrake will do nothing. So we do not have to worry about your copy."

"I'd forgotten all about it, for the moment," George admitted.

"So had I. But then I think we must assist this poor lady, and then I remember. But it is your property, George. I can only suggest that you sell it to Mr Sheldrake. That will satisfy his friends. There is no fear that the curator will ever know that Mr Sheldrake was connected with the transfer of the Manticora."

Mrs Sheldrake was gazing owl-eyed and open-mouthed at them. Her face was tear-streaked and she was speechless. If Mum could see her now, George thought, she'd never believe it was the same person. For the first time, George felt a bit ashamed.

"I'll give it to you, if it's any good." he said at once, Vernon sighed.

Mrs Sheldrake began to speak very rapidly, the words tumbling out.

"But it's not possible. You can't have a copy. There isn't one in the whole world. Everybody knows that. Craigmyle would never let anyone make a copy. Once he allowed it to be photographed, but that was ages ago, when he lent it to that exhibition, and it was a very poor photograph. You'd almost think the Manticora had moved – it came out all blurred and patchy however many times they tried. Once he allowed a drawing to be done for a text-book. You know that Mr Sheldrake has never let anyone near it, except to show it to those few friends. Whatever possessed him, I'll never understand … "

She jumped up.

"Where have you hidden it? Take me there now. Let me bring this copy to Mr Sheldrake, give it to him now, put him out of his misery."

"You must sit down. Calm yourself," Vernon said. "We cannot go so fast. First we must wait until the Manticora has gone, to be quite safe. For me to be quite safe. My client must never know about this copy, or my profit is halved. It is worth money, George, what you have done. You ought to put a price on such work. But anyway you will want to go

162

with Mrs Sheldrake when the time comes, you will want to see how well your copy looks in the place of the original. You will allow yourself that satisfaction?"

"No. That's the last thing I want," George said firmly, but inwardly shuddering. "I never want to set foot in that room again in my whole life. If I saw that cabinet again, I think I'd have a heart attack. It's horrible enough when I dream it all, as if it's never going to stop happening."

He turned to Vernon.

"It will be all right now, then, if I bring my copy to you, to keep in the safe? Better than keeping it in my locker at school?"

"Certainly. Much better, now we do not have to worry. I can keep it out of sight when my customer arrives. And that is what you must do for the future, Mrs Sheldrake, if I may give some advice. When you have this copy that George is so kind and foolish to give away, you should tell Mr Sheldrake to put it back in this cabinet and only to let his friends see it from a distance, when they ask. You should tell him not to encourage them to ask and gradually they will lose interest. They will come to forget the Manticora. In time, he will forget it himself."

"Never, never. We never will," Mrs Sheldrake exclaimed. "It's cruel to make him wait. If you could see him you wouldn't have the heart."

"I'll bring it here next Saturday morning," George said, shutting out the sound of her pleading. "I'm not coming to this shop, either, except when I've promised to. And when the real Manticora has gone, Mr Vernon can telephone you to say come and fetch the copy. I should only like to see it go, so it must be a

Saturday morning, please, because I want to be there. It will be my last Saturday morning in the shop. The real Manticora will be far away. You'll take my copy and that will be the last I shall see and hear of everything and everyone. I shall be rid of it all at once. I don't want to wait any longer than Mr Sheldrake for that to happen."

"But it will take weeks, George. I know about Vernon's customers from the Continent. They won't move until every detail is arranged. They don't dare to leave a loop-hole anywhere."

"That is correct," Vernon replied, almost proudly. "They cannot be too careful. There is much at stake. But this one is the cleverest of them all and the most experienced. I also am anxious for the Manticora to be safely across the Channel. I hope in two weeks' time from now I have news."

"Two weeks!" Mrs Sheldrake cried out in protest. "Too long. Mr Sheldrake will have a breakdown before then. He won't last two more days."

"But you must tell him there is hope. You can tell him that George is making this generous gesture."

George didn't like Vernon's sarcastic tones and cynical grins, and they made Mrs Sheldrake lose control again. She began to laugh hysterically.

"He won't believe me. If George made it, how could it be any use? It won't be any good. It won't convince anyone."

She stood up again, still laughing and crying. Vernon seized hold of her arm, rather brutally, and pushed her towards George.

"I have seen this copy. I guarantee Mr Sheldrake will be satisfied. I have never let you down when you

164

have come to me for advice. Remember that. And now show the lady out, George. That will be a part of your duties here. Also, as a relation, I am sure you will want to look after her."

He bundled Mrs Sheldrake out of the door and gave her a push down the corridor towards the shop. George followed, and managed to hold up the curtain for her as she passed through. He heard Vernon slam the office door.

He waited for Mrs Sheldrake to walk through the shop to the door, but she tottered a few steps and sank into one of the leather armchairs. She kept looking in the direction of the office as if she could hardly believe that Vernon had shoved her out in such an undignified manner. George stood by the chair, He didn't know where to look or what to say. However hard he thought about Mum and the house, he couldn't help feeling he deserved to be called a scoundrel.

"This is what it will be like," Mrs Sheldrake was moaning, more to herself than George. "Disowned by everyone. At the mercy of that crook we've employed for years. Why did you do this to us, George? What can you want with all that money? And Vernon would never give anyone a fair price, let alone you."

George realized that she hadn't listened to his reply, when she'd asked him the same question in Vernon's office. It wasn't any use trying to reason with people in that state. Mum always said about Polly's tantrums "she's past talking to". Mrs Sheldrake was still attacking him.

"Money won't make you happy, George. Look at us. We'll never know another contented moment. For a man in Mr Sheldrake's position to betray Craigmyle's last wishes and instructions is unpardonable. I don't think you understand what a terrible thing he has done. We'll never be able to hold up our heads again. I'll have to give up my lectures. Everything."

George wished she'd shut up. It was difficult to go on being sorry for someone who was so sorry for herself. He was glad Mum wasn't like that. She had enough to shout about, too. Perhaps that was what was the matter with Mrs Sheldrake. Her life had been too easy so she couldn't take it when something went badly wrong. She'd only had two worries as far as George could tell – her Matthew marrying their Polly, and now this Manticora misery. Each time she'd broken down. She ought to have some of the things to put up with that Mum took in her stride. Not that Mum would ever have the worry of Dad doing anything wrong. He wouldn't even be tempted. Might make a change if he was. George didn't know how to stop himself having these deep thoughts. Any minute now and he'd be having one of those earnest discussions with Polly. He knew what she'd say. "Growing up at last." Perhaps that was it. Whatever it was, George didn't like it. Who'd have thought he'd ever have been so concerned in his mind to be fair to Mrs Sheldrake? He wanted to be helpful to her now.

"Where have you left your car?" he asked.

"Nowhere."

"Did you come in a taxi? Can I get one to take you home?"

"No. I walked. We all have to be secretive these days, George. You began it."

"That's not fair," George replied indignantly. "How was I to know that Mr Sheldrake was … "

"We won't discuss it any more," she interrupted him. "And you can't do anything for me. Anything at all. You can't make up for your wickedness. Why, oh why ... and to think I thought we were just going to be friends ... that Matthew would be pleased ... "

She began to sniff again and looked for her handkerchief. It was crumpled into a ball and already soaking wet. George couldn't explain all over again about Mum and the house and Polly and Matthew and Robin Hood and all that – it was too embarrassing. And she wouldn't listen. She was too busy groaning and sobbing and telling him what a horror he was. It was useless to talk to her about the copy. He'd have to leave that to Vernon. He walked quickly to the door of the shop and out into the street. Fortunately, a taxi was cruising by. George shouted to the driver. Vernon would say this was part of his duties too. He held open the door and called to Mrs Sheldrake. When she saw the taxi waiting, she pulled herself together and marched out of the shop, totally ignoring George.

When the taxi had driven off with Mrs Sheldrake safely inside, George went back into the shop. Vernon was standing there, waiting. He greeted George with the familiar cynical leer.

"A good morning's work for your first morning. You learn a lot, but you don't learn enough. Imagine giving your copy to them. How can I explain to you how foolish that is, what a simpleton you are? Imagine yourself in front of the goal, and nobody in front of you from the other side, and you don't kick the ball and score."

"Of course not," George said. "I'd be offside. It's

you that's daft not to know a simple thing like that."

"Perhaps I am out of my depth," Vernon admitted, "but I should like to try to knock sense into you. Think what you could buy for the new house. I have become interested in your house and family, George. I should like to meet them all. See your mother again."

"Not likely," George said fervently. "I'd like to knock some sense into you, but I'm sick of explaining why I don't want any extra money, that I know you're swindling me over the Manticora. You'd never understand. I'm not giving away the copy because I'm sorry for Mr Sheldrake. And it's not to ease my conscience. It's for Matthew."

"Yes. I do understand. Their son. And this Polly is your sister. I understand only too well. I too have been snubbed by the Sheldrakes. I am glad you make him wait. You have a little fun torturing them."

"Speak for yourself," George said. "I want to make them wait long enough to make sure there's no mistake about the house. There mustn't be the smallest loop-hole – like your clever customer and smuggling the Manticora out of the country. I'm waiting for your cheque to be cashed and the contract to be signed and all that sort of thing. It's all got to be settled before you hand over my copy. I know you'll keep it in the safe – you won't risk me confessing to the police if anything goes wrong for Mum. I'm not like Mr Sheldrake. I wouldn't be scared to face the music if you tried to cheat me."

"Ah, but you're not a company director, a man with a reputation to worry about. You haven't got a wife who cares deeply about her status in the world and impressing her friends. Imagine how much they would pay to save all that, their whole way of life, George. Thousands of pounds. And you are *giving* it to them."

Vernon was so upset that George couldn't help laughing. Anyone would think he was losing the money himself.

"It's no laughing matter," Vernon said very sadly, and then added, "This Matthew, he must be a very good chap?"

Nineteen

George didn't say another word. He suddenly couldn't stand being in the shop for another minute. He wished he was at home, where they'd all be planning another super day working at the new house. He was sick of the fabulous Manticora. He wanted desperately to be at home, with the kids tearing about, and Dad down in the yard with the van, and Mum waiting for him in the kitchen. But there'd be nobody there by the time he got back. They'd all have gone to Dulwich. Mum was leaving him a sandwich. He wasn't going to ask Vernon any favours, such as letting him off early. He was astounded when Vernon said:

"Time to lock up. One o'clock. This morning has gone quickly. Don't expect it always to be like this."

"Two more weeks isn't always," George said.

George wished he could take the copy out of his locker that very afternoon, but he knew he must be sensible and wait until next Saturday morning. He'd collect it first thing, on his way to the shop. He wasn't going to have it around in his bag at home, on the Friday night. Vernon would have to put up with it, if he was a bit late. He could hardly believe what had happened, now that he was out of the shop and alone at home. He was supposed to have joined the others, if he had time, but he didn't feel like going to the house. He felt as if he might give himself away, blurt out something about the Sheldrakes. He needed a quiet half hour to himself to recover. He was glad that Polly and Matthew arrived in the evening just as all the family came home. They didn't stay long. They'd only come to say how Mr Sheldrake was getting on.

"He's much the same," Matthew reported, "but my mother says she can manage perfectly well on her own. They actually thanked us for coming."

"As if they meant it, what's more," Polly added. "And guess what – Mrs Sheldrake actually kissed me goodbye."

"Wonders will never cease," Mrs Fowler said.

George wished they would. He'd had enough of wonders, especially the biggest wonder of them all. Mr Sheldrake a thief too! One thing was certain. George would never be tempted again – not after this shattering Saturday. He was relieved for once that Mr Fowler refused to talk about the Sheldrakes. He didn't exactly turn his back on Polly and Matthew, but told Tom and Sid to push off and do their homework in case they thought life was one long holiday, and ordered Phil and Henry to bed early, after their exciting day. Dad always made everyone do their homework regularly, but it was always Mum or George who had to help the others, now that Polly had left home. George went into the bedroom with the four boys. Polly and Matthew took the hint. He heard them rushing down the stairs. He stayed in the bedroom. He felt extraordinarily tired himself. And he didn't want to talk to Mum and Dad about the house until that Saturday morning, in two weeks' time, when he would never dream of the Manticora again.

The next week was a lifetime, but Saturday morning came at last. School opened at nine for the free study and orchestra. George was there, waiting for the caretaker to unlock the gate, along with a small crowd of other boys, some carrying instruments, and others waiting for their form master to turn up to take them to the Science Museum to see some new model. George dashed into the metal-work studio, but not, as he had expected, by himself. Several other boys came in with him. George knew them vaguely – mostly from the fifth form. One of them was usually the runner-up in the competition. He'd forgotten that they'd be coming at the last minute, as usual, to finish in time. The entries had to be taken to form masters at the beginning of the last week of term. Judging went on all that week and the winner was announced in front of the whole school on breaking-up day. Tom and Sid were already saying they were fed up with hearing George's name read out, although they'd hardly been in the new school a couple of years.

Two of the boys came over to George's bench. He quickly pushed his bracket into the middle of the space he kept cleared, giving a quick glance at the clock. There was no chance of cheating in this competition, because everyone had to submit a preliminary sketch at the beginning and these were pinned up over each bench. Some of the finished articles didn't look anything like the first rough drafts on paper, so there was still an unknown and unforeseen factor to make the result exciting. In any case, it would be impossible not to know what the next chap was doing, while he was using the same machines. Not

like putting your arm round an exercise book to stop
people like Chepstow looking over your shoulder and
copying.

The two boys who came to talk to George were
making an ink-stand and a flower-pot holder. The
one who was doing the holder was called Kenyon.
George didn't know the other boy. This holder was an
openwork frame, with a serpent climbing up it, in the
drawing. The serpent had turned into a spray of ivy,
when Kenyon came to making it, and he'd just
decided to paint the veins on the leaves white and put
a white china flower pot inside the frame. George
thought Kenyon might win this year.

"Why don't you put a plant in the pot as well," he
suggested. "Ought to look first rate. Not a flower –
one of those things with lots of green leaves that grow
indoors."

Polly had gone through a phase of putting them on
all the windowsills, until Dad found an earwig in his
sandwich-box.

"Thanks," Kenyon said. "I will. You have some
bright ideas now and then, Fowler."

He ought to know, George thought to himself, as
he tinkered with his bracket, wondering if he'd have
a bright idea this minute to get his copy out of the
locker without being seen.

"Not finished yet?" the other boy asked in surprise.

"You've been over here working often enough,"
Kenyon said.

That shook George. He thought he'd had a fool-
proof alibi, was becoming expert in a life of crime,
and then some innocent like Kenyon could give him
away with a simple remark. He'd have to wait until

they had gone before he attempted to remove the copy from his locker. Vernon would be wondering what on earth had happened to him. George suddenly became conscious that Kenyon was staring at him, rather like Mrs Fowler did when she complained about his trances.

"It went wrong," George said to Kenyon. "I had to start again from the very beginning. I don't even know if I'll be able to finish in time to hand in. There's been a lot going on at home, too. We're moving."

They believed him. As Mrs Fowler had said to Vernon, anyone would think he was a born liar. George was beginning to despise himself, instead of patting himself on the back as he had anticipated. The two boys moved back to their benches. The others who had come in were only tidying out their lockers. They soon went. George kept trying not to look at the clock. What should he do? Leave it to the Manticora as usual. The other boy flung down his ink-stand on the bench, swearing and cursing. He was making a tray with fixed stands for the ink and was trying to mould the stands to curve outwards at the top but they kept going straight up into the air like tubes. Kenyon offered to help him, but he said he was going.

"I'll come with you," Kenyon said. "I'd never be here on a Saturday morning if it wasn't for making up for lost time. You coming, Fowler?"

"Not yet. I'll have a final crack at this object."

"Leave it," the other boy said. "Give someone else a chance this year."

"I think Kenyon'll win anyway," George replied.

"Your holder's all right," he said to Kenyon. "From the drawing I thought that serpent was going to be too heavy for the frame. Good thing you changed it."

"Changed itself," Kenyon said, but pleased with the compliment. "Cheero."

George was alone. He didn't take the copy out at once. He gave them time to walk to the main gate, to forget something and come back. He remembered what Kenyon said. He wanted to go to the door and look out to make sure no one was about, but anyone might be watching him while he thought he was being so careful and cunning. He sat at his bench for another ten minutes, and then grabbed the copy, wrapped in the handkerchief, and made a dash for it. He was an hour late at the shop. Vernon was waiting in the middle of the shop. He looked pale and anxious. Without a word he dragged George into the office, and without a word locked the door. George gave him the copy and watched him open the safe.

"Tomorrow my client comes for sure," he said to George. "Sunday is a good day for our business. Perhaps you would like to have a last look at the real Manticora?"

"I don't need to refresh my memory," George said.

"You are still troubled by dreams? Perhaps next Saturday morning, when I arrange for the Sheldrakes to fetch the copy, you will be free. Who knows? Until then, I shall put your copy and the Manticora side by side. I feel it is the proper thing to do. It is an honour for you, George. Those Sheldrakes will be humbled, you will see."

"What time will you ask them to come?"

"You'd like it to be as soon as you arrive? What do

you take me for? If I must pay your wages for the whole morning, then you must be here for the whole morning. Not an hour late like today while I am in fear and trembling. And now that I think of it, you must give the shop an extra thorough sweep and dust, to make up for your lateness. And next week I make you clean the window, while we wait for the Sheldrakes."

"Suits me," George said.

"I think it does. I think we suit very well. If you change your mind about an apprenticeship. Later on. I can wait. Three, four years. My offer is always open."

Twenty

Another week to wait. Another week of not being able to concentrate on anything, of expecting something to go wrong every minute, of counting the hours, and of not being able to feel any interest at all in the house and the preparations, of expecting Matthew to turn up to say his father was in hospital, most probably in a coma. Sometimes George thought he'd rather steal a Manticora every day than have to go through these in-between times when he had to wait for the next thing to happen and not let anyone suspect that he was waiting. Mum was beginning to notice that he was avoiding being left alone with her, in spite of being absorbed in working out endless sums about curtain measurements and then trying to convert them into the metric system. Dad kept telling her there'd be no such thing as yards and feet and inches by the time she was ready to put up curtains. He was saying or doing something stupid several times a day. He began to understand how Mr Sheldrake must be feeling about this Saturday morning of release.

Vernon was amazed at the energy with which George tackled the shop window. He kept coming out of the office to watch him, but George was too busy gazing out of the window as he cleaned it, watching for the Sheldrakes. They were half an hour early. George had expected they might be. He'd wanted to start off for the shop soon after dawn himself. They came in a taxi and when Mrs Sheldraké saw George at the window, she smiled and waved. George led the way down the shop into the office, as Vernon had instructed him. Mrs Sheldrake was almost kind and jolly – quite changed. She was like the sort of mother you might have expected Matthew to have, if you hadn't known different. Mr Sheldrake looked like George had felt all the previous week. He nodded curtly to Vernon as they all entered the office and then stood silently by the desk, very white and on edge, while Mrs Sheldrake talked to George.

"I know now why you took the Manticora," she said. "I wasn't particularly interested when Matthew first told me about your new house and Mrs Fowler's legacy. I was too concerned about my husband to pay much attention to anything else, frankly. But I've had the opportunity to think things over, told myself a lot of home truths about myself as well as about Polly and your family, George. And I'd like you to know that I truly believe that, if it weren't for the unexpected complication of Mr Sheldrake and Craigmyle and the curator of that museum, I should never have given you away. Never."

She stopped and looked straight at him.

"I'd have kept to myself what I knew about your coming to tea the day the Manticora disappeared – and not only for Matthew's sake."

"Even if he had not made this copy to give you?" Vernon asked, with his cynical smile.

"The copy!" Mr Sheldrake stepped forward eagerly. "Where is it?"

"And Mr Sheldrake agrees with me. He's quite converted. He thinks Polly ... "

Mr Sheldrake was thinking of nothing else in the world except George's copy of the Manticora. George could hear him breathing quickly and sharply while Vernon turned to the safe. Slowly and deliberately, Vernon placed George's copy of the Manticora in the centre of the table with the dark cloth, and turned on the spotlight. Immediately, Mr Sheldrake seized it with both hands to take a close look. Mrs Sheldrake sank on to her knees beside him, level with the table. There was complete silence for several moments.

Then Vernon came and stood next to George.

"You see," he said. "What did I tell you? They are struck dumb."

Mrs Sheldrake looked up at them.

"It's incredible. How an amateur, a schoolboy … "

George was having rather a shock himself. He was taking a proper look at Mr Sheldrake, sitting under the light. He wasn't at all what George had expected. George had imagined a tall thin man with that sort of elegant grey hair you see in the advertisements for old brandy with people playing chess, with silk cuffs sticking out of the ends of their black jackets with velvet collars. Mr Sheldrake was short and fat and dressed like some of the new masters at school – purple shirt, pink flowered tie, soft leather jacket and ankle boots to match. Must be his Saturday morning get up, George decided. Even Dad wore a coloured pullover on his Saturday morning off. It took a bit of getting used to, Mr Sheldrake's appearance, when you'd had such a clear picture in your mind of what someone was like. But Mr Sheldrake had put the copy back on the table and was holding out his hand to

George and saying "congratulations". If only he could tell Mum!

"It haunts the imagination, the Manticora," Mr Sheldrake said, very quietly. "Even a man like Craigmyle thought of nothing else all his life. But you need never give it another thought, George. Your giving me this copy is the end of the affair, as far as you are concerned. For me it is the beginning. It's made a different person of me, George. I might almost say a new man."

"Rot," George said, looking away, only to find Vernon still smiling at them all cynically. "It might look all right at a distance, but my copy's only made of old rubbish."

"That's not what Mr Sheldrake means," Mrs Sheldrake interrupted, and George wished once again that he could tell Mrs Fowler about this morning. What a stupid remark, as if he didn't understand what Mr Sheldrake meant.

"It's a most accurate copy in every detail," Mr Sheldrake confirmed, glad to be spared any more embarrassment himself. "The size is absolutely correct." He picked it up and balanced it in his hand and then put it down again. "I should think the weight is nearly the same, too. These bits of glass in the tail may not be jewels, but they're the right colours and the right shapes. Finicky work that. Excellently done. I'd never have thought of using scraps of bone for the ivory teeth. Embedded in sealing wax aren't they, George? The blood red line of those vicious lips, as if it had just devoured its prey."

"Just like my nightmares," George admitted.

"And the gold has that ancient look. I've no idea

how you managed that. In fact you have a great deal of talent, George. I could place you in a very good occupation in this kind of work, if your parents wished. I should like to help."

"No thanks," George said. "I've already turned down one offer from Vernon. I never want to think about antiques or thousands of pounds again. I never want to see any of you again. If you want to be nice to the Fowlers at last, you can concentrate on Polly. I'm going home now. My idea has won. I've achieved what I set out to do – the rest is nothing to do with me. I stole one thing, like Matthew's godmother's picture you told me and Mum about that first afternoon, and I've sold it for just enough to buy Mum her dream house."

None of the adults spoke. George opened the door of the office. He turned back to look at them. They were gathered round his copy on the table. The spotlight was still on it. Was it his imagination, or did his copy look a bit like the real Manticora at last. Not so harmless. He wished Vernon hadn't shut it up in the safe with the real one. As he went out of the shop he laughed at himself. What was he worrying about. It was all over.

Twenty-one

George ran up the tenement stairs, whistling. When Henry rushed to open the door, there was a marvellous welcoming smell of fried fish and chips. George's favourite meal. A good omen. He was even more pleased when he saw that Polly was cooking it. Polly's potato chips were the best George had ever tasted anywhere – better than Mum's and better than any shop or café. Matthew agreed. The kids had already had theirs, as there wasn't enough room for everyone round the kitchen table all at once, but they were sitting around on the floor, anxious not to miss any talk about the new house.

Matthew and Mr Fowler were having an earnest discussion about the best way to insulate the attic.

"You'll never be able to climb that tall ladder," Mrs Fowler said, "let alone carrying rolls of insulating felt. You've no head for heights."

"Don't worry," Matthew said. "That'll be one of my jobs. George can help. He ought to be terrific at hauling himself through that narrow trap-door. Later on, you could widen it a bit, and get a fixed ladder. You'd find it easy then."

Mr Fowler agreed instantly. He and Matthew were getting on like one o'clock these days. One of Mr Fowler's mates at work had given him an old lawn mower and Matthew had shown him how to mend it. They were taking it to the house that afternoon and

Tom and Sid were going to launch a full scale operation on the garden. Phil and Henry were going to help Matthew sandpaper one of the wooden floors upstairs, which Polly said would look much better polished than covered with carpet. Mr Fowler and Matthew began another discussion about whether to use a red lead undercoat on the metal windows in the garage. George supposed they'd discovered at last that they had the practical approach in common. He could have told them that ages ago.

Mum and Polly were still talking about curtains, above the delicious sizzle of frying. At last Mr and Mrs Fowler and Polly and Matthew and George sat down at the table.

"Glad you're here in time," Mrs Fowler said to George. "You can help us decide. We've been having an argument about who to invite to the house-warming."

"House-warming!" George exclaimed. "Hadn't you better get moving-day over first?"

"Don't tell me you'll turn out like Dad in the end," Polly said, ladling an enormous helping of chips on to George's plate. "You're usually the first to join in when Mum's imagination runs riot, and here you are calling her to order. Just like your father. Makes a change."

They all laughed, but Mr Fowler said,

"We might as well discuss it now as later. We're all here together and that makes a change too."

"Now, Dad! You can't put the clock back. Just when I thought you were getting used to the idea that I'm a married woman."

Polly ladled another large helping on to Mr

Fowler's plate. He smiled happily at her, and at Matthew. George felt more comfortable for a moment, almost as if he could believe that the Manticora had done some good besides buying the house. Then Mr Fowler said,

"Mr Basil Vernon will be the guest of honour, naturally."

"Oh no, not him," George protested vehemently. They all looked at him in astonishment.

"I thought you'd taken a dislike to him," Mrs Fowler observed.

"That's neither here nor there," Mr Fowler told them severely. "Of course he must be present. He's the family trustee."

"What did you think of him?" George asked Mrs Fowler. He found he could talk about it openly, now he'd got rid of the copy for good.

"I wasn't in a fit state to think about him as a person, not that morning," Mrs Fowler replied. "As far as I was concerned, he was Cinderella's Fairy God-mother and the Bank of England rolled into one."

"My parents know someone of that name," Matthew said. "Antique dealer."

"It's not the same person," George said hastily. "I mean it can't be. Our Mr Vernon's nothing to do … " He trailed into silence, as he realized what he was saying, and also that Mrs Fowler was giving him a queer look.

"A lot of us about," she said to Matthew. "Mr Fowler was certain there'd be hundreds of Vernons turning up to share the legacy. Aren't you glad you were wrong for once?" she said to Mr Fowler, laughing.

184

"All the same," he replied, "perhaps we shouldn't push ourselves forward. He's a busy man. He might prefer to remain a business acquaintance."

"Business acquaintance!" Polly rocked with laughter. "You'll be calling in Mr Sheldrake about your stocks and shares next."

"That's exactly what Basil Vernon is," Matthew said, "the one I know that is, a business acquaintance of my father's. His antique shop is in Bayswater."

"Is it?" Mrs Fowler said, giving George another queer look. She turned to Mr Fowler. "Of course we must ask him," she said. George had thought at first that Mum was going to protect him, even if she suspected anything bad, when she had turned the conversation away from antiques. She seemed to have changed her mind abruptly but decidedly. He was uneasy.

"And Aunt Jessie," he suggested, with a meaning look. "She'll have to be there. If it hadn't been for Aunt Jessie you'd never have thought of this particular house, would you, Mum?"

George knew she hadn't forgotten their little deception they'd organized in Vernon's office – how to explain to Dad why they already knew about the house in Dulwich. He thought she wouldn't want Vernon dropping bricks about that, but she didn't take the hint.

"Of course. So that's Mr Basil Vernon and Aunt Jessie," she replied, as if she was purposely putting them together to show George she wasn't going to be drawn into any more deception. George's appetite deserted him.

"Eat your chips. They'll get cold," Mrs Fowler said.

"You're not sickening for anything are you? Seem to have been a bit off colour lately."

George hastily stuffed another mouthful in and mumbled something through his chewing.

"If you don't think it's a cheek," Matthew tentatively interrupted, "I'd like to suggest someone."

"After all the work you'll have put in on the house by the time we're ready for a house-warming," Mrs Fowler said, facing away from George, "I should think you could bring who you liked without asking."

"Don't know how we would manage without you and Polly," Mr Fowler admitted.

"You're doing us a favour," Polly said. "Matthew is in his element. He might pretend he's only an engineer, but he has some pretty sensational ideas on interior decorating."

"Will you invite my mother and father?" Matthew asked shyly. "I think your house-warming might be just the right time and place for us all to make a fresh start and let bygones be bygones."

There was a total silence. Tom and Sid and Phil and Henry made a dash for the bedroom. Another Sheldrake row. They didn't want to listen in the middle of the thrill of moving. They'd all been sitting quietly on the floor, eating an apple for pudding, and drawing pictures of the house to take to school to show their friends. Phil and Henry were making a Christmas card of theirs, to take to their teachers. When they had gone, there was an uncomfortable pause. The kids began a game of what sounded like lions versus tigers at feeding-time in the Zoo. George envied them. He wouldn't mind letting off steam himself.

186

"We're not going on our knees," Polly said to Mr Fowler, "but think it over. Since Mr Sheldrake has been ill, we've managed to change the relationship, open it up at last. I think they'd like to come and I think you ought to say yes, Dad."

"If you think so, Polly. You could always make me behave like someone else. Don't expect me to make a fool of myself at the party though."

"I shan't expect Mum and Mrs Sheldrake to weep on each other's bosoms, or you and Mr Sheldrake to clap each other on the back and tell each other funny stories," Polly said. "But it will be a beginning, a step in the right direction, that's all."

"No it's not all," George burst out. "It was my legacy as well. Mum always does what Dad says, but I ought to be asked what I think. I don't want them to come. I'm not going to let them come. I won't … "

Hadn't he finished with the Manticora ever. If Vernon and the Sheldrakes came to the new house it would be as bad as having the Manticora there.

"What's come over you?" Polly asked.

George hadn't the faintest idea what had come over him. He looked helplessly at Mrs Fowler. He hadn't discovered until that very second that getting rid of the copy had been the climax of the fear and suspense he had been living with ever since the day of the first visit to the Sheldrakes, when he'd had his idea. He'd felt he could manage on his own all the time something was happening, but now it was all over, he'd folded up. He'd start blubbering like a girl if he wasn't careful. This must be what people meant when they talked about an anticlimax.

Twenty-two

Mrs Fowler spoke to Matthew, without looking at George.

"When the time comes, I shall be glad if you'll ask them. We can't go on sweeping our feelings under the carpet like this, thinking we've cleared everything up. That's no way to live – difficulties need facing up to. All kinds of difficulties, not only this one."

They were all silent again. It was turning into a gloomy meal. Then Polly tried to make a joke.

"You'll be glad you asked Mrs Sheldrake. She'll bring a fantastic present."

"Not an antique, I hope," Mrs Fowler said.

Matthew laughed.

"I'll make sure she doesn't. I've got my eye on a set of non-stick saucepans with heat-resistant handles, enamelled in just the right shade of blue to go with that washable paper you've chosen for your working area in the kitchen, Mrs Fowler. Jolly expensive, but that won't matter to Mother. Trust me. I flatter myself I'm rather good at choosing presents."

"A bit too good sometimes," Polly said, getting up. She yelled at the kids in the other room. "Look sharp and get ready. If we're taking you out to Dulwich in the Mini, be downstairs in the yard in two minutes flat."

The kids were going with Polly and Matthew. Mrs Fowler and George were following in the van with

Mr Fowler, after he'd collected the rolls of insulating felt.

"Shall I come and help with the felt?" George asked.

"No need. It's bulky, but quite light. You help your mother clear up and I'll wait for you down in the yard. I'll be about twenty minutes."

He went downstairs with the kids. While Polly was fetching her coat, Matthew stood in the kitchen.

"Been to any more lectures lately?" he said idly to George.

"Lectures?" Mrs Fowler asked sharply.

"You don't mind if I let it out now?" Matthew said to George. "It'll be something to talk about at the house-warming. Make my father feel less constrained."

"I couldn't be bothered to go on with it," George said, trying to sound as if he didn't care that Matthew hadn't kept the secret.

"Go on with what?" Mrs Fowler asked.

"He went to one of Mother's lectures once," Matthew said. "Don't you remember him saying he'd like to know more about her stuff after you went to tea that afternoon? I promised not to say anything in case you all laughed at him, but I'm sure it doesn't matter now. You've all got too much else to think about."

Polly came into the doorway. She looked rather worriedly at Mrs Fowler.

"You all right, Mum? All this excitement. Too much for you."

Mrs Fowler had sat down at the table. She was swaying slightly.

"Silly," she said. "Thought I might faint. It's worn

off already. You go now. George'll take care of me."

Polly and Matthew reluctantly left, when she reminded them that Mr Fowler would be back very shortly. George and Mrs Fowler were left alone in the kitchen. Neither of them made any attempt to clear away.

"You promised not to ask," George said. "You promised if I bought your dream house … "

"So I did, but I never expected, I never thought … George, is it something awful? Don't you want to tell someone? I'll share the burden, George, not because I'm frightened to lose the house but because good has come apart from the house. We're going to be friends with the Sheldrakes just in time, George. Polly's going to have a baby. Matthew says it'll be lucky to have five uncles all at once. It'll be nice for us all to be friends. But it won't be nice for you, George, to keep to yourself whatever you've done, whatever's happened. Let me take the responsibility."

George hesitated, but only for a moment. He closed his eyes to think, but all he saw was the Manticora, come just in time to remind him. It was his own idea. If he was stuck with the Manticora for life, it served him right. He stood at the sink, and looked down at the chipped and cracked inside, at the cold water tap. Mum put the kettle on for the washing up. He thought of the new sink unit at the new house, of the constant hot water. He guessed Mum was thinking of it too, thinking not long now. He sat on the backless chair by the stove while they waited for the kettle to boil. They'd bought some pine benches and a table to match and a dresser for the new kitchen. He looked down at the threadbare lino. The new kitchen was going to have a tiled floor, in a pattern of blue and white flowers. If the Manticora wanted to follow him there, it was worth it.

Not that George would ever need the Manticora to keep his guilty conscience alive. Even the prospect of his own room was spoiled now. He was glad Mum and Dad and the kids were going to have the house, but he didn't look forward to it any more. He wasn't interested in choosing his own furniture, even. The whole thing had turned into a torment rather than a treat. He felt as if he didn't deserve to have anything he wanted ever again. He'd have to spend the rest of his life doing good works like Polly used to – being kind to Aunt Jessie when they lived in Dulwich, taking her out for walks in the park. Perhaps it would be better if he didn't live in the house for very long. He wouldn't stay on and take any O-levels. He'd leave school and get a job helping in a prison or something. One thing was certain. He'd never so much as take a toffee out of the kids' Saturday sweet-bag again. He was a changed character. The happy-go-lucky George Fowler was a boy he had known in the distant past.

He wondered whether Vernon and Mr and Mrs Sheldrake were troubled in their minds as he was. Of course not. The Sheldrakes would never have another sleepless night now they had his copy for an alibi. They had never been sorry for what they'd done – only anxious not to be found out. As for Vernon, he was just a professional crook. George sighed deeply. There was another tangle he couldn't sort out. He still half liked Vernon, in spite of everything. He knew he was a sad and lonely man and that he had a funny kind of fondness for the things. He seemed almost to love that prancing horse and the madonna in his shop; he seemed almost to love the Manticora for its own sake and not for the money it would bring him or as a collector's piece to show off, like the Sheldrakes.

"George!" Mrs Fowler was shouting at him, prodding him, so that he nearly slipped off the chair. "Off in one of those trances again. I don't like it. I don't like anything. I think … "

"You're imagining things," George said, grinning in a determined way, as if he was the happiest boy in the world. "Don't be daft. How could I ever get fifteen thousand pounds really? Matthew and Vernon and all that is just a coincidence."

It was safe to say that, even if he was going to meet them again at the house-warming. He knew they wouldn't have any bother pretending nothing in the world was wrong between them. Vernon was too used to being smooth and the Sheldrakes were hypocrites. For him, it would be the beginning of an ordeal he'd never get over as long as he lived.

"Trying to give me a fright?" Mrs Fowler interrupted his thoughts again. She seemed convinced. She was smiling. She picked up the old clock that would only keep the right time if it was flat on its face. "I'll make myself respectable when we've done this lot. You know what'll happen if we keep Dad waiting. You get your coat on while I fetch my things. Wrap up those fishbones in some newspaper and we'll dump them in the bin in the yard on our way out."

Mr Fowler! If he ever found out, he'd make them hand everything back down to the last teaspoon, if he didn't die of shame first. Keeping Dad innocent was going to be a life's work as well. They didn't talk to each other while they washed up and put away. George was wrapping up the greasy parcel, when Mrs Fowler came back into the kitchen. She stood in the doorway and looked round.

"The sink's stopped up again," George said.

"I can smell it from here," she replied.

A sliver of pale winter sunshine found its way across the room, making everything look shabbier and greyer than usual. Two of the neighbours along the landing started a row. Mrs Fowler and George could hear them shouting and swearing at each other, although the door of their flat was shut. Mrs Fowler looked at George with a strange, serious expression, as though she'd just heard someone was dead. She was thinking the same as him then, after all.

"I'm ready," she said. "Are you?"

For the first time since he had stolen the Manticora, George looked straight into his mother's eyes.

"Yes," he replied steadily. "I'm ready."